Shot to Death
31 Stories of Nefarious New England

by

Stephen D. Rogers

Mainly Murder Press, LLC
PO Box 290586
Wethersfield, CT 06109-0586
www.mainlymurderpress.com

Mainly Murder Press

Copy Editor: Judith K. Ivie
Executive Editor: Judith K. Ivie
Cover Designer: Patricia L. Foltz

All rights reserved

Names, characters and incidents depicted in this book are products of the author's imagination or are used fictitiously. Any resemblance to actual events, organizations, or persons, living or dead, is entirely coincidental and beyond the intent of the author or the publisher.

No part of this book may be reproduced or transmitted in any form or by any means, electronic or mechanical, including photocopying, recording, or by any information storage and retrieval system, without permission in writing from the publisher.

Mainly Murder Press
www.mainlymurderpress.com

Copyright © 2010 by Stephen D. Rogers
ISBN 978-0-9825899-0-8

Published in the United States of America

2010

Mainly Murder Press
PO Box 290586
Wethersfield, CT 06109-0586

To readers everywhere

Enjoy!
Stephen [signature]

Table of Contents

Appearances to the Contrary	1
The Big Store	15
BOGO in Aisle Three	24
Bourne Again	29
Breakdown	32
C.O.D.	36
Custody Battle at Red Creek	41
Death Buys a Burger	52
Discharged	58
Disturbed	66
A Dog Named Mule	76
Fill It with the Cheapest	88
A Friendly Game	97
High Noon	106
Inn	110
Itching for Scratch	116
Jumping the Fence	122
Last Call	129
Officer Down	137
One-Eyed Jacks	161
Packy Run	168
Pipe Dreams	174
Puzzling	191
Raising the Bar	197
Rousted	204
Sidework	210
Smoking Gun	218
Tenant at Will	225
Unweaving the Rainbow	233
Whacking for Gomez	238
Where's the Beef	246

Introduction

Despite the best efforts of writers around the globe, the mystery short story is alive and kicking. In fact, finding and reading mystery short stories has almost never been easier.

The internet has made the form available to anybody with a connection or access to one, and the ever-evolving technology now allows you to listen or download your fixes as well.

Why have mystery short stories remained so popular with all the other entertainment choices currently available? The mystery short story starts and ends with story. Things happen. Lives are changed. Justice is sought, or in crime fiction, evaded. And that's only if nothing goes wrong.

In mysteries of all stripes, something goes wrong, and how the characters respond to those challenges provides us with lessons to follow or learn from.

If you can, try not to read this book all in one sitting. I don't want to leave you riddled by riddles and murder and mayhem. Instead, pause at the given breaks and reflect on the implications of what happened.

Only when you feel that you've sucked the marrow dry should you risk returning to the scene of the crime.

Enjoy.

Stephen D. Rogers

Appearances to the Contrary

You could learn a lot about a community by analyzing how they dealt with their trash.

I'd been following this town dump truck all morning and was impressed by the number of public trash receptacles strewn across the pier, playgrounds, and parks. The town seemed committed to keeping the trash off the street.

Twice, the truck had returned to municipal maintenance to drop off its load.

Twice, the truck had been joined by a green SUV, the maintenance supervisor stopping to chat with the two guys in the dump truck, Jack Tobey and the other guy.

The other guy drove.

Jack lifted the plastic bags from the metal receptacles and swung them into the back of the truck. Unfolded empty bags into the receptacles and tied a knot to hold them in place. Jack was the younger of the pair, his green jumpsuit crisper.

Chasing empty coffee cups as they skittered in the breeze coming off the Atlantic, Jack didn't look one bit a pornographer.

Of course, I didn't look like a private investigator, or so I hoped. That was the funny thing about appearances. However much of the time they were all we had to go on, they didn't always amount to much.

My client certainly believed Jack to be a pornographer, and that wasn't something often mistaken for something else.

Putting the image of my client sobbing out of my mind, I followed the trash truck into a strip mall and watched Jack and his partner saunter into the Cape Coddage. Clams. Lunch Specials. Ice Cold Drinks.

Seemed like as good a time to eat as any.

Jack and the other guy sat at a corner table under a large map of the Cape. Neither of them looked at me, which either meant they hadn't noticed my surveillance, or nothing at all.

My stomach growled as I stepped closer to the grill.

"What can I get you?" Behind the counter waited a Caucasian male in his forties, hosting a furrowed brow of ownership. He slid an order pad front and center.

"Large spicy Italian sub, please. Toasted. Dry. For here." A steak and cheese sizzled on the grill. My stomach roared.

"Ten minutes." He ripped off the order number and pushed it across the counter. "Ice cold drinks in the cooler."

After grabbing a bottle of lemonade, I approached the corner table.

They were discussing the Sox.

"Excuse me. I'd like to talk to Jack for a minute."

His head rose. "Do I know you?"

"Not yet." I hadn't seen Jack up close until now. His face was weathered for a twenty-something, but that could be from working outside. Anyway, his eyes were clear and his face clean-shaven.

His coworker pushed back his chair and stood to face

me. He looked only a few from retirement, his face wasted away. "What'd you say your name was?"

"I didn't. The conversation is personal. Between Jack and me."

Jack's coworker tried to back me down with a watery stare.

My client's sobs were more effective.

In the silence that followed, the owner of Cape Coddage called, "Steak and cheese. Clam roll."

"I'll get them." Jack's coworker picked up his soda and brushed by me, plunking down his drink on the next table.

I sat and stuck out my hand. "Dan Stone."

Jack shook. "You seem to know me already."

"I'm not here to wreck your lunch." I smiled to prove my good intentions. "As I said, this is personal, and I figured you'd rather I didn't approach you at work."

He glanced over my head. "Thanks, Bill."

Bill handed Jack the clam roll, standing above and too close to me, a zombie bodyguard.

I tensed, keeping my gaze on Jack. "You can go now."

Once Bill sat at his new table, I relaxed. "I believe you know a Carrie Wilcox."

"Sure." Jack lifted his fried clam roll out of the cardboard sleeve. "We went out for two years."

"You broke up with her last month?"

He laughed around the food in his mouth. Swallowed. "Is that what she told you?"

"Part of it." Broke up with her after forcing Carrie to strip so you could take naked photos of her.

"Yeah." Jack dragged the word out. "I remember it a little differently. Out of the blue, Carrie told me we were done. She was starting a business with her friends from college and she no longer had time for me."

I tried to fit the two stories together. "So Carrie broke it off. That must have hurt."

"Once the shock wore off. I still haven't told my mother. She's still working on her list of baby names."

"Was Carrie pregnant?"

"Someday. I mean that's what I envisioned." Jack took a huge bite of his clam roll, filling his mouth to cheek-bulging capacity.

From the counter, "Large spicy Italian."

"Back in a sec."

I retrieved my sub and skipped the chips, already doing enough damage to my stomach with the hots, sodium, and saturated fats. The tension created by learning how much my client had lied wouldn't help matters either.

Bill watched me cross the restaurant.

Jack chewed clam. "So what do you want from me?"

"Are you still mad at Carrie?"

"What if I am? Does she have a problem with that, too?"

I shook my head, slowing the exchange before it escalated. Whoever broke up with whom, and whether or not Jack was a pornographer, I'd been hired to complete a job. "This is about some things of hers."

"I don't have any of Carrie's stuff." Jack grimaced. "She never really left that much at my apartment. I never could figure out whether I should be thankful or worry about the fact she wanted a quick exit."

"Do you think that's true?" I took a bite of my sub.

Jack's sigh seemed to account for more air than his lungs would hold. "She's a gownie; I'm a townie. Carrie will graduate and leave the Cape to conquer the world. Maybe someday I'll make foreman."

"Is that what you thought, or what she thought?"

"My break's over." Jack downed half his ginger ale. "I gotta go."

I plucked a card from my shirt pocket. "Give me a call."

"Why?" Jack crinkled his debris as he stood.

"Because if you call, you get to choose when we talk." Behind me, Bill scraped his chair back.

"Seems like we just did talk." Jack boxed his shoulders.

I swallowed the food in my mouth to keep him from having the last word. "It was a start."

Ignoring my card, Jack scurried along the wall to the trashcan and left the restaurant by the far door.

"Thanks for recycling." I slipped the card into my pocket and returned to my sub, colorful but somehow tasteless.

I waved to Jack out my car window as he left the municipal maintenance barn, waved my whole arm in wide arcs to ensure everybody noticed.

Jack frowned as he broke from the gang and approached.

"I almost didn't recognize you without the green jumpsuit." What about Bill? Why wasn't he among those leaving?

Jack stopped a couple feet from the car, his stance defensive. "What do you want?"

"We never finished talking earlier."

"I have nothing more to say." He opened his mouth

and then snapped it shut.

"How about I buy you a beer?"

"No, thanks." Jack didn't sound as though he appreciated the offer.

"An ice cream cone?" As long as he stood there listening, I'd keep casting. "There's a place just up the street. Their ice cream is hand-packed, whatever that means."

Jack's front leg twitched.

I leaned out the window. "I'll drive, or you can follow me, whatever you want. It's your choice."

Around us, the other employees had already entered their cars and left. We were alone.

Jack relaxed, his body settling into his sneakers. Then he walked around my car and climbed in. "Let's get this done."

"Done is good." I started the engine and took my time getting us to Malarky's Seaside Chills. "I didn't see Bill."

"He had an appointment. Chemo."

"Sorry to hear that." But not sorry I didn't have to worry about him coming at me from out of nowhere.

"He's a good shit."

"So Carrie tells me you have something of hers."

Jack's head snapped toward me. "I already ..."

"Pictures. She says you have pictures."

"Pictures?" There was confusion in his voice. He wasn't repeating the word to buy time. "What pictures?"

"Bedroom pictures."

Jack's squawked, an outraged swan. "You're joking. Carrie can't dictate what I think and feel. Just because she threw me out of her life doesn't mean I'm going to edit her out of two years' worth of pictures. I have a right to my memories."

"She has a right to privacy." I pulled into Malarky's, parking as far from the order window as possible, hoping to keep Jack in the car and talking. He wasn't the pornographer Carrie suspected, or led me to believe she expected. So what did that make him?

"Should I puke up every meal we ate together?" Jack's nostrils vibrated. "Give myself a lobotomy?"

I turned my back to the door, willed my body to project nonjudgmental, nonthreatening interest.

"All she's concerned with are the nude photos. She's not denying you two had a relationship."

"Nude?" Jack snorted. "Leave Carrie to remember that night. What's she think, that I sit at my computer clicking through the pictures, pining for her?"

"That's not her major concern."

Jack looked out his window. "She's unbelievable."

"I don't doubt that."

His visible ear trembled as his neck muscles clenched and unclenched. "I have half a mind to simply refuse. Where does she get off?"

"Hmm." I tapped the steering wheel with my index finger. "I have equipment that securely wipes a file. Beats all government specifications. Doesn't touch anything else."

"What would you do?" He faced me. "In my shoes."

"I'd back up my data, just in case."

Jack almost smiled. "That's not what I meant. About the photos."

"There's no need to delete them for the storage space, especially since memory is cheap. But why would you want to hang onto pictures of an ex?"

His eyes widened. "Why not?"

"Because they've lost their value to you. All they're going to do is slow down scans, slow down backup." I paused half a beat. "They even slowed your ride home today."

Jack nodded. "So what about the pictures on Carrie's computer? The ones she took of me?"

As my stomach lurched, a piece of undigested hot pepper burned through me. I winced. Shifted. "She didn't say."

"Didn't say what she did with them, or didn't mention them at all?"

"Carrie hired me to deal with the photos in your possession." That she'd lied to me changed nothing. Clients always buried as much as they unearthed.

"The pictures I took, I created them, right? That means I own them." Jack's whole body started talking, his motions animated. "It's like when my friend got married. The wedding photographer owned the negatives, not the happy couple. My friend paid for the prints he wanted."

"This is different."

"How so?"

He had to ask. Somehow I didn't think the fact that I had a paying client was enough of a distinction.

"You don't want this in the papers."

"Neither does Carrie."

I unclenched my fingers from the steering wheel. "It's true that Carrie isn't interested in spending a fortune on legal fees. That's why she came to me, so that you and I can work this out without getting mired in lawyer depositions and court dates."

"I'm not afraid of paperwork."

"What about your boss? What's he going to think about one of his employees collecting naked photographs? How's that going to look? You, the guy people see hanging around the beaches. At playgrounds."

When Jack crossed his arms, that undigested pepper shot flames up my windpipe.

I leaned forward, lowering my voice. "Listen, Jack, nobody wants this to get any more complicated than it has to be. Carrie is uncomfortable with the idea you still have those photos. Make them go away, and the issue goes away."

"Maybe I've decided they have sentimental value." His jaw muscles were so rigid his words came out clipped. "Maybe I don't want to give them up."

"Come on." I gave him a knowing smile.

"Carrie and I were together two years." He softened. "I've never felt about anybody else the way I felt about her."

"Holding onto those pictures won't bring her back."

"I know that." He was in turn defensive and defiant, as transparent as the cycles of an ocean tide. "In fact, here's my offer."

"I'm listening."

"Carrie wants all rights to those photos? Fine. She can buy them from me."

"She doesn't want the photos." And if Jack hadn't been the pornographer Carrie claimed, he was fast becoming something dangerously close to one.

"It sounds to me as though she does. Right now, they're in my possession, and Carrie wants to change that. End of story."

"I understand ..."

"Fifteen hundred bucks and they're hers. You call her up, and you tell her my terms." Jack reached for his door handle. "And I want it in cash."

I watched Jack examine the flavor board posted next to the order window.

"Carrie? Dan Stone. I've met with Jack."

"I told my friends, you da man." Her voice grew less distinct, as if she'd moved the phone to talk to somebody else. "Mumble, mumble, mumble." Celebratory whoops. Then she was back. "So, like, thanks."

"Hang on. We have a complication."

"Can you deal with it?"

"That depends. You want the photos. Jack wants fifteen hundred."

"Does he really expect me to pay to see nude photos of myself?" Female laughter erupted in the background. "I don't think so."

"I'll see what I can do." Jack walked toward me licking an ice cream cone. White with dark smudges. "One other thing."

"I'm kind of busy."

"Jack said you had photos of him. I could use those to leverage a trade."

"Long gone. I'm not the only person who uses my computer, you know." More background laughter.

"I'll be in touch."

Seeing Jack just outside, I did a quick massage of my stomach.

He opened the passenger door and dropped into his

seat. "Okay if I eat in your car?"

"Go ahead."

"So do we have a deal?" He left the door open, keeping one foot on the pavement.

"My client understands your position, but payment is out of the question. We still feel, however, that this can be handled so everybody comes out ahead."

"How do you figure that?"

"Jack, I don't believe money's the answer. Carrie did you wrong, and sticking her for fifteen slips of paper isn't going to change that. Buy something with money you get from Carrie, and it's going to be haunted."

Jack didn't respond, his mouth busy cleaning up ice cream that was already starting to melt down the cone onto his fingers.

He heard me, of course. His free hand picked at the seam of his jeans.

I let him chew on my words as he licked.

Then, apparently satisfied that he had the ice cream situation under control, Jack faced me. "Fifteen hundred."

"I hear you, Jack. But it's not going to happen. Instead, you're going to get something better."

"Like what?"

"We go back to your apartment, and I get two pieces of equipment out of my trunk."

"What kind of equipment?"

I held up a hand. "When we get inside, you print out a single picture of Carrie. I use the first piece of equipment to wipe the files. You then use the second piece of equipment to shred that picture. We then celebrate your freedom, however you want."

"You're talking, what, a party?"

"If that's how you want to celebrate. A party. A couple drinks. Split a pizza and watch a game. It's your choice, your reward."

Jack shook his head and returned to his cone. "I don't know."

"Think back to the first time you had ice cream. You were probably pre-verbal. It was strange looking. Cold. You could feel the cold coming off it, and you weren't so sure you wanted to let that stuff touch your lips." I paused. "But then you got that first taste. And the world was a better place."

"You should do a commercial for them." He tipped his head toward Malarky's.

"I wouldn't know what to charge."

Jack stared at me as if trying to judge how I meant that, and then laughed. "Charge them three grand. And then split it with me."

I tap-punched him in the upper arm. "How's that ice cream?"

"Good. You owe me ten dollars."

"Ten dollars? I've got to stick to places that pack their ice cream by machine."

"You said you were buying, and I tip well."

Raising my eyebrows to indicate he'd gotten the best of me, I chuckled. "I'll give you the money when we get to your apartment."

"You're not going to try to talk me down?"

"Of course not, I promised." I paused. "Besides, the ice cream falls under reasonable expenses, for which I get reimbursed."

"You mean from Carrie." Jack grinned.

"That's correct." It was a pleasure to deal with a person

who didn't need everything spelled out.

"Let's get this done. Then we'll celebrate, Carrie's treat, right?"

"Carrie's treat."

Since that day, I'd seen Jack around, picking up other people's trash, fitting empty bags into the receptacles. Didn't see him long enough to say hello or send a salute, just out of the corner of my eye.

Then he called. "I thought you might get a kick out of this."

"What?" I rolled my chair far enough from my desk that I could swing back and forth, my feet crossed at the ankles. The online asset search could wait.

"A friend of a friend knows one of Carrie's friends."

"Should I be drawing a flowchart?"

Jack laughed. "He said that he said that she said that Carrie ran with that business idea."

"And?"

"Why Carrie wanted those pictures back? She and her two friends from college, they started their own porn site. Soft porn, featuring a lot of sea, sand, and skin. Or so I'm told."

"You haven't checked it out?" My chair squeaked.

"Old news. Just like you said. Anyway, I thought you'd enjoy hearing that."

"Thanks for the call, Jack."

You could learn a lot about people by analyzing how they dealt with their trash, the litter they produced as they marched through life's parade.

The detritus.

The jetsam and flotsam, washed up onto shore, left behind ensnared in seaweed as the waves withdrew with a soft sucking sound.

Or not.

I pulled myself closer to the computer and the interrupted asset search. Resumed my hunt for treasure.

The Big Store

Carl lowered his voice. "Before I say anything about the job, I have to know whether you're in or out."

Richard and Sully looked at each other over the table. "In or out of what?"

"I can't say until I know."

The two men agreed that they were in.

"Good. We're going to keep this tight. Don't tell your friends. Don't tell your brother-in-law. Don't tell your wife."

Sully leaned forward. "Carl, I'm not married."

"Then don't tell your girlfriend."

"I don't have a girlfriend either. Not any more. Me and Alicia, we split up."

"I'm sorry to hear that."

"She said she needed someone with a more secure future, as if theft wasn't the fastest growing crime in America." Sully shrugged. "But what can I say? She already made up her mind."

"When we finish dividing the take from this score, she'll realize she was a fool to let you go."

The waitress sighed. "So do you guys want drinks or not?"

Carl held up three fingers. "Beer, draft."

"Any particular brand?"

"Surprise me." He shook his head as he turned his

attention to his team. "Anyway, we're going to set up a big store."

Richard winced. "I don't know, Carl. The big stores, they all seem to be going Chapter 11."

"Yeah. I saw this debate on PBS about whether the economy was a good thing. It really made me think."

Carl held up a hand. "No, a big store is a type of con. Instead of going somewhere to steal money, we're going to create a situation so that the mark brings the money to us."

"That's a whole 'nother ball game then."

"Mark who?"

The waitress cleared her throat. "You guys want a pitcher?"

"I wasn't talking about a real ball game. It's a figure of speech."

"Your beer. A pitcher is cheaper than three mugs."

Carl stared at her. "You still standing here? Just bring us the three beers. We'll save the money on the tip."

He waited for her to stomp away before he continued. "Not only is the mark going to bring us the money, he's not going to go to the cops afterwards."

"Why not?"

Carl grinned. "Because the money is dirty. He reports it missing, the cops slap the cuffs on him."

"You're a genius. Everybody says it."

"Who are we talking about, anyway?"

Carl sniffed. "Michael Vallente."

The two men froze. "The mob guy?"

"Do you know anyone else sitting on as much secret cash? Come on fellows, trust me. I've got everything covered. I even have someone inside. Nothing can go wrong."

The men relaxed, Richard laughing and Sully flipping his fork into the air.

"That's a relief."

"For a second there, I was worried."

As Sully leaned down to pick his fork off the floor, Richard asked Carl how they were splitting the money.

"Even-Steven."

"But there's three of us. That's an odd number."

"I'll take two shares which brings it to four."

Richard nodded and then slapped Sully's hand. "Hey, don't you be switching forks with me. You dropped it, you ask for a new one. Here she comes now."

The waitress placed the three mugs on the table.

"Can I get a fork?"

"Sure, but you'd quench your thirst faster if you used a spoon. How about a straw? We've got bendy ones for the kids. You get to choose whether you want red, blue, or green."

Carl snickered. "Is the rest of you as smart as your mouth?"

"Why would someone with a master's degree in statistics be waiting tables?"

"You tell me."

"The company I worked for decided employees were an unnecessary expense."

Sully slapped the table. "See you guys, that's what I was talking about. Local companies just can't compete with the global warming. It's all over PBS."

Carl took a sip of his beer, waiting for the waitress to bring a fork from the next table. "How would you like a piece of the action?"

"Michael Vallente action? No, thanks. I'd rather be

broke than dead."

"What's your name?"

"Taking into account the large capital letters printed on this plastic tag, you're pretty safe calling me Helen."

"Well, Helen, who said anything about Michael Vallente?"

"You did. The bar's only about two feet from your table." Helen faced the bar. "Hey, anybody who thinks these guys will live twenty-four hours past their little adventure, please raise your hand."

Nobody at the bar moved a muscle.

Carl coughed. "Nothing can go wrong."

Hands shot up into the air.

Helen rolled her eyes.

"So are you in?"

"No. You'd probably pay me less than you'd pay the men and then stick me with menial tasks. And when all was said and done, Michael Vallente would kill me just as dead as if I was an equal partner."

Carl drummed the tabletop. "You drive a hard bargain. Okay, we'll do our own laundry. The thing is, we could use your statistician skills to make some charts."

"What kind of charts?"

"If I knew that, I could do them myself."

"Look, I'm on the clock here. You want to talk, you come back after closing and make me an offer."

"I'll do that."

As soon as Helen left, Richard grabbed Carl's arm. "If we cut her in, that brings it up to five shares."

"I'll take another one to make it even."

"You're a fast thinker."

Sully shifted in his seat. "So what's the plan?"

"It's a law of nature that you can never be too rich. We're going to hook Vallente and reel him in easy."

"Easy sounds good."

"First thing we do, we staple a hand-lettered sign to the telephone pole outside his house: Earn $3000 to $5000 per week working from home."

Helen laughed from behind the bar.

"When he calls, and he will, we tell him we're in the herbal supplement business and offer to take him on as an associate."

"Why don't we just keep the $3000 a week? That's pretty good money."

From the kitchen, Helen shouted, "A hundred and fifty-six grand before taxes."

"Because we don't actually have any product. Once he signs up, you two will order from him using a variety of identities to the tune of two thousand dollars worth, each."

"It sounds to me like Vallente is the one getting richer."

"That's the key to good con. Right when Vallente is starting to have delusions of grandeur, we move on to the second stage. Timing is everything."

"What's the second stage?"

"We tell Vallente we want to go e-commerce, but we require seed money for hardware and programming. If he made four grand in three days with no advertising, just imagine how much he'll make once he's on the Internet."

"A hundred and fifty-six grand starts to sound like peanuts."

"So how much you gonna stick him for?"

Carl sat back. "Two million three."

"Why not two million even?"

"It sounds better this way. We'll tell him the three

hundred thousand is for consultants."

"Maybe we should just become consultants."

Helen stopped at the table. "You guys want another round? A pitcher? Maybe a shortstop?"

"What's a shortstop?"

"The player between second and third base."

Carl said they were doing just fine. "Right now, I think we could use a little privacy."

"It's down the hall on the right."

"Thanks." Carl waited for Helen to leave before he continued. "Any questions?"

"What if Vallente doesn't go for it?"

"We're out the cost of a flyer and some staples."

"And what happens if he does?"

"We'll set up a meeting, tell him to bring cash because our lawyer is worried about a paper trail linking an herbal supplements company to someone who has a majority stake in the regional meat-packing industry."

"So you don't mention the mob connection."

"I don't even whisper it."

Sully shook his head in admiration. "You don't miss a trick."

A heavy hand dropped onto Carl's shoulder. "Hey, fellas. You having a good time?"

Richard paled. "Mr. Vallente."

"Beer cold enough? Glasses clean?"

"Sure. Everything's grand."

"From time to time I like to visit my establishments, talk to the customers. Mind if I join you?"

Sully stood and offered his chair.

"Thanks." Vallente sat and turned to face Carl. "The bartender told me you were here tonight. Planning anything big?"

"Just a surprise party."

"Am I invited?"

Carl grinned. "If I told you, it wouldn't be a surprise."

"You're a funny guy." Vallente looked at Richard and pointed at Carl. "He's a funny guy."

Richard nodded and gulped.

Vallente continued, "There was this fella once, he thought he could rip me off until I had him whacked. He was a funny guy, too."

Carl shrugged. "Maybe you just bring out the best in people."

"Maybe I do." Vallente banged his fist against the table. "And then other times, I just have them killed. Who knows? Maybe dead is the best they can be. At least it keeps them honest."

"You can't overestimate the importance of honesty."

"No, you can't." Vallente pushed back his chair and stood. "Why don't the three of you do yourselves a favor and rethink your little party. Helen!"

"Yes?"

"Another round here, on the house."

"Thank you, Mr. Vallente."

"You're welcome. I'm a better friend than an enemy. Remember that."

"We will."

"See that you do." Vallente took two steps away from the table when someone called his name.

He spun and cocked his head in surprise. "Mr. Ponzi. What can I do for you?"

"Mikey. I just had a disturbing call. A woman not your wife told me you'd also taken up gambling with money.

My money."

"There must be some mistake." Vallente cleared his throat.

"That's what I thought. So I went to your office, and you weren't there. You're supposed to be there."

"I received a call myself …"

"We checked the safe, and it was empty. Mikey, what'd you do with my money?"

Vallente opened his mouth twice before speaking. "Empty? That's not possible. I was just there fifteen minutes ago, and I saw the money with my own eyes."

"The woman on the phone said you'd say that. She also said I'd find you here. When two out of three prove right, I'm going to trust her on the third."

"I don't understand." Vallente breathed deeply. "I don't know why, but somebody is feeding you bad information."

"Perhaps. We'll talk about this some more and see if we can't clear up the confusion. Why don't you wait for me outside. I'm going to use the restroom."

Vallente paused before nodding. "Certainly, Mr. Ponzi. We'll get to the bottom of this."

"I sincerely hope so."

Vallente straightened his shoulders before leaving the bar. Mr. Ponzi watched him go. Everybody else watched Mr. Ponzi, the room completely silent, and the door closed behind Vallente with a solid thud.

Three shots rang out followed by a squeal of tires.

Mr. Ponzi shook his head as he started down the hall toward the restrooms. "We live in dangerous times."

Carl leaned forward and switched back and forth between Richard and Sully. "Both of you screw out the back door before the cops get here. Keep your mouths shut and stay out of trouble. I'll be in touch."

Richard and Sully disappeared through the kitchen to the left of the bar. The rest of the patrons followed.

Carl smiled when Helen finally arrived with his beer.

"Here you go. I see you already ditched your two friends."

"They flew away like little birdies, and I'm sure they're already singing our version of tonight's events. You talk with your brother yet?"

Sirens added their song to the ambiance.

"Just now. That's why the drink took so long. A rough count makes it at least a hundred and fifty big ones that Vallente was holding. Not bad for a night's work."

"I told you nothing could go wrong." Carl raised his beer and winked.

BOGO in Aisle Three

She was waiting for him in canned goods, walking up and down the aisle, placing an occasional item in her cart so she wouldn't appear suspicious. She still didn't understand why he wanted to meet here, but he was the expert, and he did.

She added Mandarin oranges to the stack.

"Hello?"

She looked up to see an attractive man, mid-thirties, neatly dressed. She faltered. "Do I know you?"

"We spoke on the telephone."

"Oh, yes." Already she was acting the fool, but she had pictured a different type all together. She had prepared herself for someone coarser, someone who had been scarred by his experiences. "How did you recognize me?"

"By your cart."

She glanced down at the haphazard collection of cans, not a single thing from any other aisle. "Someone would think I was expecting a storm."

His eyes were reassuring. "Are you?"

"Yes. I believe I am."

He lifted a tomato paste. "My favorite."

"Keep it. I have plenty."

He smiled, flipped the can into the air, and caught it as if he did so every day. "Thanks."

"What happens now?"

"Well, if you're done here ..." He flipped the tomato paste again. "I could use some pasta."

"No, I meant, you know."

He was silent until another shopper selected three cans of corn and left the aisle. "Tell me. Was this a good idea?"

"What?" She had already countered her second and third thoughts. She didn't know whether her resolve could survive his playing devil's advocate.

"Meeting in a supermarket. I've only recently expanded my business to normal people and thought this would be a more comfortable place to talk."

"Am I normal people, even after wanting someone killed?"

"There's nothing more normal than that."

She smiled. "Perhaps, but to go through with it? I mean, sure, drug dealers and the like have no conscience, but who else would actually hire a hit man?"

"Cashiers from the ten items or less register."

She forced herself to laugh. "Seriously."

"Seriously, very serious people who take themselves too seriously. I'm seeking a more level-headed clientele."

She sniffed. "Next you'll be telling me that hiring a killer is a sign of level-headedness."

"Certainly. The overly emotional try to do it themselves, as though murder was as simple as hanging a door."

"Have you ever hung a door?"

"No, but I shot one once." When she didn't respond, he continued, "Loosen up, that was a joke. There's a reason we're here instead of some back alley."

They stopped talking long enough for two shoppers to pass, one going each way.

She suddenly quivered. "I'm not sure. Does he really deserve to die? God knows he's made my life miserable, but I'm only one person. Is that enough to justify killing him?" She leaned forward over her cart. "I must sound silly to you."

"No. Sort of refreshing, actually. By the time I'm usually called in, it's all bluster and righteous indignation."

"Do you understand what I'm saying?"

"I do." He returned the can of tomato paste to the shelf.

"Well?"

He shrugged. "I can't make the decision for you. From what you say, it does sound as though you might be trading one hell for another if you go through with it."

"I have to wonder."

"Listen, you don't need to decide this now. Consider it a canned option with a long shelf life. Today, tomorrow, next month, it's all the same."

"I'm afraid if I do that, the can will be pushed to the back of the cupboard. Someday I'll find it and be reminded of all the times I'd wanted that exact thing but had to make do with a poor substitute."

"Would it help if we walked?"

She shook her head. "I'd only be distracted, lulled by the onslaught of marketing campaigns. People shop so they won't have to think, and think is what I must do. I must. He always called me indecisive."

He licked his lips. "I could meet you here tomorrow, if that takes some of the pressure off you."

She pointed at a can on the shelf, swung her finger back and forth between it and a larger size. "Eight-ounce or twenty-ounce? The twenty-ounce has a higher price tag, but when I compare the cost per ounce, the larger can is cheaper."

"Actually, the larger can is still more."

"That's it exactly." Now she saw what they had all been trying to hide. "Say I only require eight ounces. It wouldn't make sense to buy the twenty-ounce can for the lower unit price if I threw out the other twelve ounces."

"Meaning what?"

"Meaning ... kill the bastard. Look at what he's reduced me to." She reached for the safety of her cart, the cold metal, the molded plastic.

"Are you sure?"

"Yes." Wasn't this meeting over yet?

"There are no returns if you later change your mind."

"No."

"No, don't do it?"

"No, there are no returns. Receipts are meaningless. No refunds, no exchanges. When you purchase someone's death, you have reached the pinnacle of consumerism."

"Perhaps I'm the one who needs to reconsider."

She grabbed his arm. "You can't abandon me now. Not when I'm so close."

"Close?" He gently disengaged her grip.

"Yes, to making my final decision."

"I thought you had."

She felt faint, heard an announcement go over the store's PA system but couldn't decipher the words. "Tell me again that I'm normal."

"I'm no longer so sure."

"Try to sway me, convince me to say yes. Promise me my life will never be better. Guarantee your work." She held out a trembling hand. "Offer me a discount, a coupon, a sale."

"How about buy one hit, get one free?"

She froze and then slowly drew herself to full height. "You are too cruel for words."

That said, she pushed the cart with her collection of cans to the first open register, paying for the items with unmarked bills.

Bourne Again

I watched the cars speeding around the rotary, paid special attention to ones that veered off to head over the canal.

Despite the "Cape Cod Tunnel" stickers that locals bought to infuriate the tourists, there were only two ways off the Cape. Since I couldn't see him going out of his way to take the Sagamore Bridge, I was waiting in the IHOP parking lot at the foot of the Bourne.

He was a redheaded man who drove a white Chevrolet and if he were going to come this way he'd do it in the next twenty minutes.

He claimed to have received Jesus but his wife suspected that any ecstasy he might be experiencing had less to do with conversion to Christ than with an ex-girlfriend in Wareham.

"Gateway to the Cape," my client had snorted into her coffee. "More like Gateway to the c ..."

A white sedan cut off my reverie as sharply as it did a rental truck in a last ditch effort to change lanes before passing the exit for the bridge. It wasn't him.

The advantage of a rotary was that if you missed your target, you could simply circle around and try again. People didn't, though. They drove as if their first shot was their last, using horn, finger, and unflinching bulk as they risked all. To hell with the consequences.

Across the road from the restaurant was a State Police barracks. I'd never seen a trooper posted at the rotary. In the time it took to write up a single moving violation, five more occurred. Who could keep up with the paperwork?

Another white car approached, a young woman whiplashing enthusiastically to the song on the radio.

I shifted in my seat.

My client couldn't pinpoint where the ex-girlfriend lived. Postal delivery was not a given right in Wareham, and the tramp used a P.O. box as well as an unlisted number.

Why the suspicion?

Her husband had been unusually happy lately.

"Maybe he found peace."

"He found a piece all right." She reached for her cigarettes, her cracked fingernail polish complementing the nicotine stains. "She blew him once in high school, and he's pined for her ever since."

If the economy had been better or my overhead lower, I would have passed. Domestic was dirty. No matter how the investigation went, the client felt shamed, and I was the messenger who knew the truth.

I much preferred doing background checks for human resource departments, but no one was hiring right now. Reminding myself that rent was due, I agreed to determine whether her husband was lying.

She grinned through the smoke. "Then I'll really have the bastard. He thinks his life is miserable now?"

Two cars entered the rotary. The second contained the husband.

As he started up the approach to the bridge, I pulled out of the parking lot behind him.

So my client had been right about her husband skipping religious services. I admit I was surprised. Church worked as well as an affair to get him out of the house, and it was less dangerous.

Mid-bridge, the Chevrolet suddenly stopped.

I hit my brakes, and the driver behind me followed suit, white-knuckled and swearing in my rearview.

Further back, I thought I heard a crash, but in front of me the husband had climbed onto the roof of his car and raised his hands in supplication.

Some people found happiness in attaining, others in letting go. My client was wrong after all. Her husband had been going to church just long enough to reconcile himself.

As I grabbed for my door handle, he lowered his arms.

I had one foot on the pavement when he leaped over the safety barrier.

I reached the walkway as he hit the water below.

Time returned to normal, and I heard the traffic again, drivers scrambling from their cars, screams.

From experience I knew I'd have no trouble breaking the news to my client, writing the report, calculating the bill. The image of her husband's peaceful resolve, however, that would haunt me.

I gripped the railing and stared down at the canal, cursed a blue streak.

Like I said, I hated domestics.

Breakdown

She was parked along the wrong side of the road, facing into traffic, probably having chosen the location because of the dark trees that crowded the lane she'd been traveling.

Her face was pale and swollen, the nondescript features molded and remolded by kneading hands even as I watched.

Then I was past.

Ours were the only two vehicles in sight, hers shrinking rapidly in my rearview mirror.

Would she want me to turn and stop, offer assistance, a shoulder? Had she become overwhelmed while driving and pulled to the side, half-blinded, or had she specifically sought the privacy afforded by this deserted stretch?

"Mom, can you come over and stay with Danielle? ... I just need to go out. ... Alone. ... Thanks."

What would she say when her mother arrived? Would there be time and opportunity for words, or would the two women pass silently, each alone with a singular version of the event? Would Danielle fuss? Wave from the window as her mother drove away?

Perhaps Danielle had been sleeping.

"Thanks for coming Mom. ... Alan is gone. He packed up and took off. ... It's Danielle's arm. I know I told you the break was an accident, and it was, but now he doesn't trust himself. He's not a violent man. ... No, he never hit me. He never hit Danielle either. ... That doesn't matter. ... What's important is that he's left, and he says he's not coming back."

Alan sold commercial real estate. He specialized in restaurants because he understood the particular needs of their owners. Only one in three restaurants survived the first year. When Alan helped select the site, shared his advice on matters ranging from vendors to signage, the odds rose to one in two.

He often pictured himself running a restaurant but couldn't bear the thought of the hours he'd be kept from his family. Absentee owners were often the main reason for the failure of their dream. Alan understood the responsibilities.

Danielle gathered bottles of nail polish from her mother's bureau, transporting them to her father's den in an old slipper she found under the bed. She made four trips. She then opened the desk drawer that held his files and poured the nail polish over the folders.

She still cannot answer why she this did this. She shrugs and says the colors were pretty. She is not capable of relating her actions to seeing her father run over the doll she neglected to bring into the house.

When Alan entered his den to see his daughter destroying his records, he snapped. So did the bone in Danielle's arm as he tried to yank her away before she caused any more damage.

"Gin, I can't stay. I can't bear to see Danielle, knowing what I've done, what I'm capable of doing."

"She's forgiven you."

"She's three. It will be years before she begins to

comprehend what happened. Even then, she won't be in a position to forgive me, even if she does."

"Alan, it was an accident. We've been through this."

When Alan was in fourth grade, he saw a classmate shot by a student on a rampage. Explanations for the dead and wounded did little to mend shattered misconceptions, even less to bring Alan's friend back from the dead.

"I broke her arm. Nothing can change that."

"Whatever she may have lost in terms of trust, she shouldn't have to lose her father, as well. She loves you."

"Someday she'll appreciate my sacrifice."

"No. She won't."

What did he take with him when he walked out the door? Did he fill a suitcase with clothes? Did he empty a box of Christmas ornaments so that he could carry the barest of necessities to the car? Had he planned ahead and rented a trailer? Had he hired movers? Had a mover, carrying the last piece of furniture out of the den, kicked the cover from a bottle of nail polish, causing it to roll across the floor of a now empty room?

Where was Danielle during all this?

How soon afterwards did Ginny call her mother?

"Mom, can you come over and stay with Danielle? ... I just need to go out. ... Alone. ... Thanks."

Did Ginny cry as she drove to the most secluded spot she could imagine, a road bypassed by faster connections? Did she fill the car with loud music in an attempt to distract, to keep the earth-moving sobs at bay? Did she bang her fists against the steering wheel? Did she remember to signal her turns?

Did a small part of her hope, as she recklessly crossed the opposite lane, that the tears in her eyes kept her from seeing on oncoming truck?

Had she seen me approach, draw even, pass? Had she tried to meet my eye?

Had she watched my car shrink in the rearview mirror as I had watched hers?

How would she have reacted if I'd knocked at her window? Would despair have become fear and then fury or something else?

While I'd been thinking, I'd been driving. I now sat at a speaker, listening to a disembodied voice ask if I wanted French fries with my order.

Was the young woman at the microphone the possible future of Danielle, bravely assembling her sense of confidence and self-worth after years of destructive behavior, finally putting the past behind her, losing herself in the minutia generated by an active life?

Was there a manager, a father figure, who monitored her success rate for suggestive selling, who compared customer/fry ratios across the various employees who strapped on a headset?

Was a quarter raise riding on whether I requested the fries?

I hadn't stopped for her mother, couldn't stop her father, but consumption was within my grasp. For the price of French fries, I could make a difference in someone's life.

Did her arm ache when the barometer changed, when she didn't get enough sleep, when she witnessed a father and daughter together?

"Would you like fries with your order today?"

"Yes," I said. "That would be wonderful."

C.O.D.

I should have been sleeping, but I couldn't.

Four out of six nights this past week, I'd been woken about this time by the sound of a racing engine followed by a thud and then hoots and hollers as the pickup drove away.

Boys will be boys, I was told.

"Damaging a mailbox. Isn't that a federal offense?"

The Sheriff shook his head. "School's getting out. The boys are just blowing off a little steam."

"I traced the plates. These boys of yours graduated two years ago. Barely."

"Well, aren't you the little private investigator."

I should have been sleeping, but I lay in bed ramrod straight, beads of sweat bullets on my brow, fingers clamping the edges of the bed as if I was holding on for dear life.

The alarm would go off in two hours so I could beat the sun to an early-morning surveillance. I'd spend the rest of the day tracking down the usual paperwork and tomorrow night face this same hell, a little more exhausted.

Three weeks, I'd been burning the candle at both ends. The last thing I needed was to have my poor excuse for sleep disturbed by a bunch of hooligans.

"This doesn't have anything to do with your brother, does it?"

The Sheriff sat back. "My brother?"

"You just have the one." After those two, their parents would have drowned any subsequent male offspring at birth.

"John works nights pumping gas, about as dangerous a job as a man can have, near as we are to the highway." The Sheriff pulled at his right ear. "He applied to work at the school department, but something odd happened."

"He lied on the application."

The Sheriff leaned forward. "Is that some kind of, what did you say, federal offense?"

Pressing my thumbnail against my leg, I managed to keep my voice level. "The school pays me to verify what the applicants claim."

"I see. That's very interesting."

Finding the boys parked behind the gas station with a case of beer, I talked to them myself. Of course, they knew nothing from nothing.

They didn't know where I lived. They didn't know the Sheriff or his brother. They didn't know why the previous owner of the pickup hadn't fixed the dents in the front end, but they were saving up money to do it right.

When I said I was going to set up a camera to catch the perpetrators in the act, they laughed. They were still laughing when I climbed into my car and drove away. I could see them howling in the rearview mirror as they threw empties in my direction.

"Perhaps I should just talk to the Postmaster."

The Sheriff smiled. "If you do, tell him I'll be late for the game tonight. The missus wants me to look at a new dining room set. Me, I'd like to know what's wrong with the one we have."

"Perhaps the lawful owners stopped in and recognized it."

His lips thinned. "I imagine there's a lot more opportunity for a man of your profession in the big city."

"I like it here just fine."

"You just might end up liking it a lot less."

My eyes felt as though they were nestled in sandpaper-lined sockets, as if the fluid that coated them had been laced with low-grade acid.

Four nights, the pickup had struck, and I was out ninety-six dollars trying to guarantee the postal carrier would leave me my share of bills, checks, and the regular assortment of junk.

Today I spent a two hundred and twelve.

"Sheriff, I think we should be able to resolve this peacefully before things escalate."

He grinned. "After all, we're both grown men, both of us interested in justice."

I bit my tongue, nodded.

"You're the private dick. What do you suggest?"

"If the boys discover some other way to sow their wild oats, I'll forget about the incident." I paused. "We'll call it even."

The Sheriff raised his hands. "What's in it for me?"

"You?"

"I suppose you're asking me to hunt the boys down, give them a little pep talk, play activity director. That's probably three or four hours I don't have to spare. That means using overtime to complete my regular work."

"And just what's your overtime rate?"

"It's not so much an hourly figure as it reflects how much of an asshole someone is." The Sheriff grinned.

I spent this afternoon digging a deep hole, building a temporary support for the steel shaft, pouring in quick-dry cement. Four hours later, I slid the plastic mailbox post over the shaft, disassembled the support, and replaced the sod.

Both boys lived at home, and I left a message telling them it was in their own best interest to stay there tonight.

I should have been sleeping, but the tension from waiting twisted exhaustion all out of shape. I was not merely over-tired. I was somewhere on the far side of sleep where deprivation tasted exquisitely brittle, where the line between reality and hallucination was barely visible and tended to move with a life of its own.

The Sheriff placed his hands behind his head. "I figure ten thousand will cover my expenses. That'll leave you enough to rent a moving van, buy some boxes, and throw yourself a farewell party."

I heard an engine in the distance.

My eyes ached with a purity approaching the sublime.

Except for fingers that had become claws, the rest of my body had disconnected from the musculature necessary to move it.

The pickup was roaring closer.

"Sheriff, I don't think you're interested in helping me."

"Only in helping you out."

I sucked in my gut and used the momentum to raise myself to a sitting position, swinging my legs up off the bed. I slowly extended my fingers and tried to flex my toes.

The sound of the racing engine vibrated the house, and then the force of the crash shook the clock off the table.

I pulled on pants and shirt as I staggered from the

room and toward the front door.

What I wouldn't give to lie on the couch and sleep through the day.

The pickup was wrapped around the steel shaft, the engine dead but ticking from the heat. The passenger door was open, and a body lay on my lawn.

The right front tire, lifted up off the ground, spun in the moonlight.

As I approached the wreck, the body moved, and the boy stood carefully, shaking his head.

I grabbed an arm and twisted it behind him, pushed him up against the house, slammed him into the siding. "Whose idea?"

He must have led with his chin, because I could hear him choking on his blood, couldn't understand a word he said.

I turned him around and jabbed him in the chest until he met my eyes.

Certain I had his attention, I repeated the question.

He started to shrug and passed out instead, folding into a bundle at my bare feet.

I crossed the lawn to what was left of the pickup, making a wide circle around the accident to avoid glass and shards of metal.

The driver was pinned to the back of the seat.

He was dead.

"Ten thousand dollars? Sheriff, boys will be boys, but men will be men."

I returned to the house, sat on the front stoop with my head in my hands.

At some point, I must have fallen asleep, because I woke to flashing lights.

Custody Battle at Red Creek

"You know I don't like working on custody cases." The only thing more foolish than trying to argue with an attorney was arguing a point that was inconsequential. I didn't know whether this early morning meeting made me the bird or the worm, but I didn't become a private detective to turn down work.

"I could say that my client needs you to find some inflammatory things about the father, if she means to keep her son, but I won't stoop to that. You wouldn't be swayed by the wholesome picture represented by a mother's love."

Laughing out loud, I saluted the good attorney. "Nor by the tears that well up in her eyes when she talks about junior, the catch in her voice when she utters his name." Shaking my head, I leaned back in my seat. "You know how these cases are. The parents say that they're fighting for the child, but they're really just battling each other, using the child as a weapon. Custody cases are as nasty as they get."

"I'll just say this about the job." He brushed an invisible piece of lint off his suit sleeve. "The father's attorney has retained the services of Dan Discher."

I let loose a low whistle. If I attempted to stay away from custody cases, Discher succeeded. That hyena succeeded in everything he did, whether it was stealing my wife or the golden-goose client that took me six months of smooth talking to land. "Discher doesn't touch anything but corporate cases now that he has Javelin Networks."

"The way I understand it, the father's attorney snagged Discher by mentioning that the mother hired me and that I usually hire you."

Grunting, I looked out the window and imagined that I saw Discher falling past it. Having won every round so far, why was he so eager to step back in the ring? He didn't have anything to prove. He was the one with the prime client and the belle of the ball.

After counting to ten, and then to twenty, I agreed to take the case. Discher didn't have anything to prove, but I did. The chance for revenge didn't escape my attention either.

Out came the yellow pad, and I was soon scribbling away. One thing about working with attorneys was that they were prepared with the necessary information, no hemming and hawing. Time was money, and they appreciated that fact as well as I did.

Since the end client was the mother, I called her as soon as I was alone. While I knew that the attorney had been thorough giving me what he had, I couldn't be sure that she gave him everything.

"I'm the detective working for your attorney, and I wondered if you had any additional information. Maybe you forgot something, or you were too embarrassed to mention it at the time."

"Well, one of his deadbeat friends called last night. I guess he didn't know we split."

I grabbed the pad. "Just what did this friend say?"

"That he'd be fishing at Bluff Point today until noon

and that the creel was full, whatever that means."

I glanced at the clock and saw that I had three hours. "The creel is where the fisherman stores the catch."

"Whatever. Fishing was never my idea of good time. Is this going to help me keep my boy?"

"Maybe. I want you to call the father and pass on the message."

A whine crept into her voice. "Do I really have to talk to the S.O.B?"

"You want to keep your son, don't you?"

Disconnecting, I found a map and traced the length of the river until I found Bluff Point. The road didn't come closer than a half mile, and I figured that if the father was going to do anything worth hiding, then he couldn't have chosen a better place to do it.

Folding the map into my pocket, I grabbed my camera, the telephoto lens, and the video camera that hadn't begun to pay for itself. While it seemed that everything that happened in the world was captured on videotape, my purchase had as yet produced *nada*.

In the car and driving toward the river, I had little to think about besides Dan Discher. I had been in business for two years when Discher rolled into town. He was flashier, dirtier, and perhaps even better at the job than I was.

While I was out nights on surveillance work, Discher wooed away my wife, who thought that his brand of detecting was going to give her a better life than mine did. While I was out days serving papers and photographing disability claims as they mowed lawns and painted houses, Discher was convincing Javelin Networks that he could better meet their needs.

While we saw each other from time to time, we had

been alone only once. This was after my wife moved in with him. I was conducting a background check, talking to a food store manager about someone who once bagged groceries there. Who should I meet in the pasta and rice aisle but Dan Discher carrying a basket filled with some of my wife's favorite things.

Discher held out a hand, "No hard feelings?"

"Not quite." My fist shot out, and he went flying, although I had to admit that he probably sustained more damage from the cans that he sent tumbling than he did from my fist.

I took a right onto Edgewater Road.

While I had thought the encounter at the food store evened things out, I knew now that it hadn't. I was going to do a better job than Discher this time, and he was going to lose.

As I reached the sharp turn that was as near as the road came to Bluff Point, I pulled over and gathered my equipment. While I didn't fish myself, I knew enough to play the part of a freelance photographer, if I was unlucky enough to walk into the father or the deadbeat friend, not that they would just shrug and go on with their dirty business.

The trail to the Point was well worn, and I couldn't tell if there were any recent footprints. I just hoped that I was here sooner than the father so that I was able to capture his meeting on film or perhaps even video.

The deadbeat friend had said that the creel was full. Since the creel didn't fill until after the day's fishing, that meant that the friend was bringing something to the meet. A charge of handling stolen goods or drugs would go far toward making sure that the father didn't get custody.

As soon as I heard the river, I cut off the path and headed toward the sun. I didn't know which way the river flowed, nor whether fishermen moved upstream or downstream, but I knew that I'd both get better photographs with the sun at my back and have less chance of being sighted if the sun was in their eyes.

The bugs started getting at me, and I silently agreed with the mother that fishing was no way to have fun. Of course, I wasn't fishing, I was trekking through bug-infested woods with surveillance gear, which meant that detecting wasn't much fun either.

Though I stopped every ten yards to listen for a minute, I was soon at the river's edge. Taking a long look upstream and downstream—I could tell by the way the water piled up against the rocks—I saw no one either fishing or passing illegal goods.

Putting the telephoto lens on the camera, I could see a sandy outcropping that I assumed was Bluff Point. Moving only five yards at a time, I moved closer to the spot in case the meeting happened on the other side—downstream, if it matters.

Fairly sure that I was deep enough in the woods to see without being seen, I waited for the father to appear or the deadbeat friend to come from further downstream. Trying to ignore the bugs, I let my muscles relax.

Noon came and went without sight of the deadbeat friend, the father, or even an interesting bird. Either the mother had misunderstood the message or passed it on to the father, who called the deadbeat friend with a better meeting place.

Breaking down my camera, I walked along the shore to the path and took the easy way back. When I reached my car, I saw that all my tires were slashed.

Just in case Discher was watching from the woods with his video camera, I restrained from a display of emotion and thought about revenge. I didn't know how, but I was going to get him for this. Leaving me up a creek without a paddle wasn't going to win Discher the case, and he knew it.

Discher had resorted to schoolboy tactics just to add insult to injury. Looking back, I realized that I should have asked the mother whether she knew the deadbeat friend or whether she just assumed that he was a deadbeat friend from something he said. I should have asked if she would recognize Discher's voice.

Shrugging the camera equipment into a more comfortable position, I started walking toward town. For whatever reason, it seemed like Discher took this custody case because he wanted to play cat and mouse games with me.

Did I turn the other cheek and concentrate on the case, or did I swing a two-by-four at him from behind? Perhaps if I hadn't remembered the car he drove, I would have chosen the nobler path. Then again, perhaps if I hadn't remembered the car he drove, I simply would have made a telephone call to my friend at the Registry.

I needed to make an appropriate response to Discher's move, and I thought I knew what it was. All I needed was a bag of sugar and a little luck tracking down his car. While I was aware that getting revenge wouldn't prove me the better man, the better detective, or the better human being, I knew it wouldn't hurt.

I found Discher's car after two hours of driving the rental around town, just after I promised myself that I would quit this goose-chase if I hadn't located the car in the next ten minutes.

At this rate, the custody case would be decided before I unearthed a single thing on my client's behalf. While I realized that this might be part of Discher's plan, I couldn't keep the tremor out of my hands as I sighted his car in a street lot next to an office building.

While he was inside, probably selling some company on why he could do a better job than me, I was pouring sugar into his gas tank. Then I popped open his trunk and pulled out the spare tire to leave it lying against the side of his car.

We were even, an eye for an eye. He had disabled my car and I had disabled his. Of course, his would be more expensive to repair, which didn't hurt my sense of justice.

Meanwhile, I didn't want to win the battle only to lose the war. I turned the rental around and headed back to my office to find another chink in the father's armor. The attorney had given me an employer, a landlord, and a list of friends who actually existed.

When I walked down the hallway, I saw that the door to my office was open.

I called out "Hello" as I walked through the door, hoping to disarm anyone waiting to jump me. Perhaps the father wasn't at Bluff Point because he was waiting here for me.

The small office was empty and appeared completely undisturbed. I took a moment to wonder whether Discher had slashed my tires before breaking into my office or afterwards.

A quick look found everything in order. My filing cabinets were still locked. My computer was functional.

My answering machine didn't have an obscene outgoing message. My desk drawers weren't turned upside down.

Perhaps Discher had just broken in to spook me. While he might just have done it to prove he could, the open door bothered me more than the physical act of slashing my tires.

Was he hoping that I stayed in the office worrying instead of working on the case? Was he hoping to make me snap and do something stupid? Had he left the office and tried to start his car yet?

To be completely honest, I wasn't sure what would happen when he turned the key, whether the car would run for a short time or whether the engine would immediately seize up.

I looked up at my closed door, glad at least that the lock hadn't been broken.

Opening my middle drawer, I pulled out the folder to get the telephone number of the father's employer. When I opened it up, I found a strange document on top.

It was a photocopy of a Bill of Sale. Discher had sold his car yesterday, which meant that I had poured sugar into the wrong person's gas tank.

I closed the folder and cursed Discher. He was so far ahead of me that I couldn't even see his dust any longer, not that I ever had sight of it. I couldn't believe that I had destroyed the wrong person's engine. Inside this folder was the name of the person whose day I had just totally ruined.

Now I knew why Discher had broken into my office, to leave this photocopy to prove that he had countered my move before I even thought it. I wondered if my ex-wife was helping him.

It had to be a mind-game. There wouldn't have been any information in the folder that Discher didn't already have. As a matter of fact, he probably knew enough about the father to win the case for us. I needed to hustle and get a piece of that action.

I picked up the telephone to call the father's employer and then paused. Discher could have bugged my telephone while he was here, but then, why advertise his presence by leaving the door open? Was the open door his way of taunting me, of daring me to discover all he had done while he had free reign of my office?

Was the Bill of Sale photocopy the only reason Discher had been here, or was it only the most obvious reason? How much time had he spent planning this whole thing out?

I was zero for two and there was no reason to believe that Discher wasn't going to throw me another curve.

Putting down the telephone, I decided that I had to stop simply reacting to his moves. Action was called for, and I needed a plan of my own. It wouldn't be enough to simply slug Discher the next time I saw him. That hadn't worked last time, and it wouldn't work this time.

I needed to create a plan as complex as his own. I needed to create a thing of beauty, something that would catch Discher by surprise and solve this thing for once and for all.

A half hour later, I had my plan. In case Discher had bugged the office, I walked across the street to the Red Creek, ordered a sandwich, and then used the pay phone near the bathrooms to make the call that I had sketched out.

When I returned to my seat, there was Ellen waiting for

me. That was the problem with an ex-wife, she knew where to look.

Ellen glanced at me and then stuck to her fingernails. "Did you get my message?"

"No."

"I called your office and left a message."

"I was just there ..." Discher must have listened to my messages and deleted them. "It probably got erased by mistake."

She shrugged or nodded or something. "It's just as well. I didn't make a lot of sense."

"What's up?"

Ellen took a deep breath. "I broke up with Discher."

"You're joking."

"I called to see if you were doing anything tonight."

"Actually, I am."

"Oh."

I laughed as I realized what sent Discher charging after me in the first place. He had something to prove after all. "Tomorrow, I'm free, but tonight, I have to finish an investigation. Actually, you could help."

Ellen blinked. "How could I help?"

I nodded toward the telephone. "I just called the opposing party in a custody case and told him his attorney hired a detective to investigate him."

"So. Attorneys don't like being surprised in court."

"I told him that Discher dug up so much dirt that he approached me, willing to sell the photocopies and pictures. I said the trade was happening tomorrow and that then I was willing to sell the materials to him for twice what I paid."

"Were you serious?"

"Of course not. Discher's office is fifteen minutes from the father's apartment but five minutes from here. After I videotape the father breaking into Discher's office, you can call the police and report hearing suspicious noises."

I smiled. "With any luck, the cops won't arrive before he wrecks the place."

Death Buys a Burger

"That will be a few minutes, Sir."

"I've got six bullets and a trigger finger which say it will be sooner."

The young girl shrugged and looked past me. "Can I help the next person in line?" Either the green dye in her hair affected her hearing, or I'd lost my touch while I was in the stir.

I hoped it was the dye.

Standing there like some kind of idiot, I watched the pimply kids behind the counter bump into each other while buzzers buzzed and beepers beeped. Only one guy seemed old enough to drink, and he looked like he'd been hitting the bottle since breakfast. He also had a ring in his nose.

So this was the fast food revolution I'd heard so much about. I wasn't impressed.

There used to be a diner here, The Silver Room. Steak and eggs for four bits served by a waitress named Mabel who didn't take shit from nobody. I once saw her chase a guy out into the parking lot with a meat cleaver, and all he'd done was stiff her on a fifty-cent check. She never did like cops.

"Burgers up," cracked a voice out of sight.

I wondered whether Mabel had managed to change with the times or whether she'd been thrown away with yesterday's garbage. I couldn't picture her working in this carnival surrounded by posters of cartoon characters and silly buttons.

"You're all set, Sir." Miss Green Hair pushed a tray toward me: a burger in paper, fries in cardboard, and soda in plastic. I wouldn't be surprised if that described the taste, as well.

"This is my meal?"

"Napkins are over there."

Elbowing my way through the people crowding the counter, I skipped the napkins and grabbed the booth that had the best view of the office building where Terrance worked.

The diner where we planned the robbery was long gone, but Terrance had a job right next door. Maybe he felt like he couldn't escape the fallout from that day. He was right.

A kid toddled up to my table, handed me a ketchup packet.

When did they start letting kids into restaurants? "Thanks. Now make like a witness and disappear."

His mother scooped him up, glared at me. I tried to smile, but I must have been out of practice, because she beat a hasty retreat. Fuck her.

After two bites I stopped eating. The food was as bad as I expected, worse than anything I'd forced down in prison. I'd been a good boy twenty long years, and this was my reward. While I had expected prices to go up while I was inside, I didn't think quality would go down.

Pushing the tray to the other side of the table, I thought again about Mabel. What I wouldn't pay to see her approach with my slab of rare steak, black coffee with a shot of Jack, some wisecrack fresh from the gutter.

Across the aisle, a kid started screaming.

Where did a man go to eat these days? I never thought that prison could start to look good in comparison to the outside, but it did. Sure, some guys used the front gate like a revolving door, but I never realized it was on purpose.

A plastic toy barely missed my head before crashing against the booth behind me. I kept my hands on the table. If nothing else, prison ground patience into a person. Before I'd gone up, I would never have tolerated this shit.

As it was, I had to remind myself that Terrance was getting off work soon. This was the best place to watch for him. It was always a mistake to change plans midstream.

The bank job had gone smooth as silk until someone tripped an alarm, and the cops descended like flies on a corpse. We scattered and opened fire. By the time the newspapers tallied up the score, I was behind bars, Walters was dead, and an unidentified third man was wanted by the FBI.

Through a prison guard, I slipped Terrance a single note: "Save my share." From the rumors I heard inside, he didn't.

It was understandable, in a way. The law could have been on his heels, just waiting for the right moment to strike. He might want to live it up while he had the chance.

My note, however, didn't leave much room for confusion. He should have done like I asked. After all, nobody was going to say anything about the share that Walters wouldn't be claiming.

The front doors of the office building opened, and a steady stream of suits and dresses came pouring onto the sidewalk.

Terrance hadn't aged a day.

I was out of the booth and heading for the exit when a family of four stepped in front of me to argue about who was getting what size fries. Tracking Terrance through the windows, I pushed my way past the cattle and crossed the parking lot, quickly closing the distance.

Even if Terrance did manage to slip out of my sight, I knew I wouldn't lose him. Twenty years of long gray days and longer dark nights, I'd thought of little else but meeting up with my ex-partner. I had one of those psychic connections.

Terrance stepped around a bum holding up a can, took a left into a parking garage.

I followed, waving at the guy in the glass booth. The stairwell door slammed shut, and I pulled the gun from my pocket as I headed that direction.

The stairwell smelled like prison without the bleach.

Terrance's footsteps echoed above me.

Half a flight up, I heard another door open and close.

I caught up with him on the third level.

He had his back to me, was busy unlocking a car door. There was no one else within sight, not that it would have made any difference. "Terrance."

He turned and then paled as soon as it clicked who I was. "You got out." His eyes dropped to the gun in my hand.

"I thought it was time to take advantage of this internet thing, use my share from the bank job to seed an e-commerce business. America was built on venture capital, and who am I to argue with America?"

"Look, I'm going to pay you back. I just need to get all my ducks in a row." Terrance stepped to the side so he'd have the option to bolt.

I countered the move, keeping him trapped between me and the car. "Speaking of water fowl, how does the phrase 'dead duck' grab you?"

"I swear I'll make it up to you."

"And how do you figure to do that?" I could see him scrambling for something that would keep him alive. Panic froze some, inspired others. I hoped for his sake that he belonged to the second group.

"I could deal you in. That would be perfect." He glanced around. We were still alone. "After the bank job, I went straight."

"So did I. Straight to jail."

"I took some classes, learned the business. I might have started at the bottom, but I have my own office now." Terrance stopped as if waiting for congratulations.

When none came, he coughed and continued. "I process appraisal forms for a large insurance agency. I know everything there is that's worth stealing in this town. I even know what kind of security the owners have installed on the premises."

I had to admit the situation had potential. "So what?"

He lowered his voice. "I keep a list of the best places to hit, sort of an insurance policy. It's sweet."

"Keep talking."

"The list is in my desk back at the office. I can take you there right now. I've just been waiting to put together a team. We knock them over one at a time. Bang, bang, bang. Then we split. It would be like old times."

"For some of us, old times weren't that good."

Terrance licked his lips. "Look, nothing I could have done would have made any difference, but I'm sorry you were caught."

"I'm sorry you spent my share. I asked you nicely not to."

His eyes were skipping around, looking for a way out. "A lot can happen in twenty years."

"Tell me about it."

"The past is the past." Terrance didn't realize that he was adding salt to the wound. He was talking fast now, trying to sell me. "This is better than a bank job. It's a sweet deal."

"Not as sweet as this." The first bullet flung Terrance back against his car, the second two pinned him there long enough that I was ten feet away before I heard him hit the ground.

I should have asked him first if he knew where I could get something decent to eat. I hated to break and enter on an empty stomach.

Discharged

"The Professor is here as my guest."

His three lieutenants stared at me with dead eyes. I didn't wave a greeting across the table or congratulate them on their success in evading the clutches of New Bedford's organized crime task unit, although I'm usually a pretty friendly guy.

"The Professor will be assisting me in the matter we're about to discuss." Cunningham crossed his hands over his belly. "In this matter, he speaks for me, but only in this matter."

In other words, once this matter had been resolved, they were free to dump me in the Crapo Hill landfill. The remaining two of them, anyway.

"Earlier this week, one of you three overstepped his bounds. If I'd wanted Manny capped to keep him from testifying, I would have given the order. I didn't. Now, instead of bribing an official, I'm looking at first-degree murder. The DA called me himself to gloat."

I could see why Cunningham brought me into this. The three men sitting opposite him didn't even blink.

I'm not sure why I expected anything different. They were thugs like their boss, each guilty of all the crimes available in a small American city. Three finer men had never graced the inside of a federal penitentiary, and I labeled them Slick, Eyebrows, and Wheezy to keep them straight in my mind.

Cunningham continued. "I don't need this kind of trouble, not with these upstart gangs snapping at our heels. While I can appreciate that whoever whacked Manny was just trying to protect me, the whole idea was ill advised."

Ill advised. What a quaint way to issue a death sentence. Someone outside the crime world, someone who didn't even skate along its edges as I did, being a private investigator, might think the comment innocuous. Bureaucratic doubletalk. Fluff.

Those of us in the room knew better.

One of these three lieutenants was going to die shortly, and I had the dubious privilege of pointing the finger. Me, Dan Stone, PI. Defender of widows and orphans.

I'd been chosen to play a part in this drama because I was based on the Cape and rarely worked New Bedford, never in these circles. The lieutenants didn't know who I was, and that gave me the advantage. A very thin advantage. Perhaps just thin enough to cut me from ear to ear.

"I asked the Professor to join us because I didn't feel like sending your guns to the State Police Crime Lab in Sudbury. What with their funding situation, I didn't want to wait that long for an answer." Cunningham laughed, probably imagining the day he got his hooks into that unit.

"Professor?"

My stomach lurched as I realized he meant me. "Gentlemen, I've been invited here not to make accusations, but to run a scientific test of my own design. While I didn't realize my work was common knowledge, your boss is not exactly John Q. Public."

Cunningham nodded, acknowledging the compliment.

"I've been assured that none of you have had cause to discharge your weapons within the last week. My test can determine whether you have, in fact, fired your gun recently, no matter how well you may have cleaned your firearm afterwards."

Of course, I was full of shit. I was running a bluff against three guys who appeared to have perfected the poker face. Not to mention Cunningham, who wouldn't hesitate to kill me if he learned I'd lied to him.

"Please place your weapons on the table in front of you."

They each looked to him, and he motioned they should do so.

Three guns came out and were plunked down. All were .45 caliber semiautomatics. Not the most fashionable gun on the market, but deadly nonetheless.

Starting with Slick's gun, I made sure there wasn't a round in the chamber before I ejected the clip and handed it back to him.

"As you may or may not know, when you pull the trigger of this or almost any gun, you cause the primer to ignite the propellant which creates an explosion which forces the bullet down the barrel. This process generates something called gunshot residue."

I laid three cotton swabs on the table.

"Among other things, the residue contains compounds of barium, lead, and antimony. What I've done is develop a formula that can verify the presence of a microscopic quantity of these elements. All in about five minutes."

I answered the question I knew they would have asked if they'd been free to ask questions. Fortunately for me, they weren't. Tough guys did not raise their hands in order to admit ignorance. Tough guys were morons that way.

A six-year-old would have cut my bluff to ribbons.

Next to the cotton swabs I placed a small glass specimen bottle which contained a slightly gray tap water.

I studied the three men across from me. Before I could determine who was trying to hide his response to the test results, I needed to catalogue the men's normal tics and behaviors. A person who clears his throat before speaking might be lying, unless that person typically clears his throat due to causes unrelated to the topic at hand.

"I've conducted almost a hundred double-blind experiments, and my formula has never produced a false positive. If the moistened swab reacts to the inside of your gun barrel, you can bet your life you've fired your gun within the last week."

Cunningham laughed at my turn of phrase. He could afford to laugh. He was the house, and the house always won.

I pried the rubber stopper out of the bottle and dipped the first swab inside. Capped the bottle. Slid the swab down the barrel of the Slick's gun. Repeated the ritual two more times.

"Five minutes, gentlemen."

In five minutes the average person blinked sixty times and swallowed twice, but these were not normal circumstances. I didn't bother counting the blinks or swallows, the sniffs or shifts. Instead I watched for the tell that would indicate guilt. I waited for a killer's unconscious to confess.

Which was almost funny, since it was a poker player's inability to read his opponents that had brought me to this place. I'd gone to Cunningham: discharge my client's debt, and I'll be available whenever you need an investigator. He'd surprised me by accepting the offer, perhaps even then knowing this day was coming. Perhaps he'd weathered several *coup* attempts already.

I made a show of checking my watch. How could one minute have passed so soon? My armpits were suddenly damp.

When Cunningham had summoned me to a bar in Brockton, he'd called whoever killed Manny a traitor, a traitor who'd silenced Manny only to protect himself. Outside the DA's office, only Cunningham's three lieutenants had known where Manny was being hidden. Cunningham needed me to figure out which one had pulled the job.

Since I had no interest in spending any more time with these goons than necessary, I'd quickly fabricated my formula story and sold Cunningham on the idea I could determine the killer using science.

Did psychology qualify?

Two minutes were up.

Even the pair who didn't kill Manny should have been nervous. What did they know from false positives? If I screwed this up, they're the ones who might be wrongly accused. How could they not find that thought sobering?

The fact that none of the three appeared nervous made me nervous. Just knowing he had displeased Cunningham should have put the killer on edge, but then maybe he knew something I didn't, such as he hadn't used the gun he'd placed on the table.

If that was true, I was sunk.

Eeny, meeny, miny, moe. Pick the killer; don't be slow. If you're wrong, then they will know. Out goes bang, bang,

bang.

I'd never claimed to be much of a poet, and apparently the possibility of being shot wasn't proving very inspirational.

Three minutes were up.

Even those who understood the psychology behind tells were susceptible to them. Learn to stamp out one nervous behavior, and another will emerge to relieve the pressure, greater now due to the additional effort of hiding the first.

How was my body revealing my inner turmoil? Had the others in the room spotted my tell, guessed what it might mean? Or would they simply excuse any strange behavior on my part, accustomed as they probably were to people under a great deal of stress?

One minute.

Cunningham cleaned his fingers, using the nails on one hand to scrape under the nails on the other, as if he didn't have a care in the world.

What about the killer? Was he replaying the highlights of his life? Weighing his regrets? Communing with his maker?

Perhaps he was too busy developing a plan of action. Scripting a bluff of his own. Or maybe he was betting on the long shot, gambling that science too had bad days, and that my test would fail for the first time ever.

Of course there was no saying the killer hadn't seen this coming and prepared for the eventuality.

For all I knew, he was two steps ahead of me. Maybe as soon as I announced the results of today's examination, he'd denounce me as a private investigator whose grade for intro to chemistry had hovered around a D.

Then he'd shoot me with his backup gun. Or call in his friends who were waiting just outside the door. Maybe Cunningham would do the deed himself, outraged that I'd tried to con him with my talk of experiments.

Time.

"When I withdraw the swabs from the barrels, the swab that has turned slightly blue will indicate which gun has been recently fired."

During these five minutes that had flashed by like so many seconds, I'd been analyzing the three lieutenants, watching for some indication of guilt, hoping that even a sociopath would feel remorse after betraying his boss.

There. As I reached toward the swabs, the killer revealed himself, a facial tic that nobody could miss except that all eyes were on my hand.

I withdrew each of the swabs and examined them. Once I indicated that one was slightly bluer than gray, everybody would see what they expected to see. That too was psychology.

After taking a deep breath, I nodded toward Slick.

He pushed back his chair. "No, I swear--"

"Take him away. Put him away." Cunningham watched the brief struggle impassively, ignoring Slick's claims of innocence as he was dragged from the room.

I tried to ignore the proceedings, quickly gathering the swabs and slipping them into my pocket to distract myself from thinking about the fact that I'd just condemned a man to certain death.

Whatever I might have done today, one of the lieutenants would have been marked for death. Perhaps my involvement had been the only thing keeping all three from being killed outright.

Cunningham had never been known for half-measures.

"We're even then, my debt discharged."

Cunningham smiled at me. "Yes. Until I need you again someday."

"But you said ..."

His smile became a frown without even moving. "And now I say different. You want to join the last man who forgot his place?"

"No."

"Good. When I call you, Professor, you come. Day or night, whatever you're doing, you come. Understand?"

"I understand."

He waved me away, perhaps only releasing me because he believed he held the end of my leash tightly in his grasp.

Outside, I marveled at how the sunlight tickled the shadows, how the breeze off the ocean dispelled the city's exhaust. I was alive. More than that, I'd seen my plan through to the bloody end.

By accusing Slick of the one crime he didn't commit, I'd cemented the position of Eyebrows, the traitor who would eventually take Cunningham down.

I could discharge my own debts, thank you very much.

Disturbed

I reached the front desk out of breath. "I locked myself out of my room. I left my sales figures on the desk, and I'm already late for the meeting."

The clerk smiled. "Room number?"

"Six thirty-three."

I tapped my fingers on the counter while he did something behind it. His name badge read Eliott.

Eliott handed me a plastic room card. "Your old one will no longer work, Mister Wodehouse."

"That's fine. Thanks a million."

I rushed to the elevator and paced until it arrived with a muted ding, stepped out of the way while the business travelers poured out.

Inside, I calmly pressed the button for the sixth floor.

I'd followed Wodehouse down and out to his rental. Since he hadn't returned within fifteen minutes for anything like a forgotten presentation, he was sure to be gone the rest of the day. I only needed his room for two hours tops.

With his poorly cut suit and serviceable briefcase, Wodehouse was the epitome of the dependable middle manager, predictable to a fault. I'd stood facing the closed door of the first guest to vacate and waited for just that look.

The elevator doors opened, and I turned right toward 633.

Wodehouse had walked past me like he owned the hotel, and I had to bite my lip to keep from laughing. Empty appearances were all his type could ever hope to achieve, so sad it was funny.

At the door, I pulled on my gloves before I slid the card into the slot and watched the light blink green.

I twisted the handle, stepped inside, turned the plastic MAKE UP ROOM over to DO NOT DISTURB.

First things first. I crossed to the desk and called room service. "This is Wodehouse in six thirty-three. Could you send up a bottle of scotch and two glasses?"

"Certainly, sir."

"While you're at it, we'll take two steaks, medium rare, and a shrimp cocktail."

"I'm sorry, but we're still serving breakfast."

"Of course. Do you have steak and eggs?" I opened the desk drawer, but Wodehouse hadn't put anything personal inside.

"It comes with our own hash brown potatoes and three slices of country toast."

There was nothing of Wodehouse's on top of the desk either. "Two of those then, still medium rare, and the eggs runny."

"That will be about twenty-five minutes."

"And coffee, a pot of coffee." I glanced at my watch before hanging up. I'd start the shower in twenty.

Besides the desk, the living room boasted a sectional couch, a coffee table, the ever-present entertainment center, and three large plants that had seen better days.

I went through the door to the bedroom.

There was a double bed under an odd painting, two end tables, and another entertainment unit set on top of a bureau. Wodehouse was a messy sleeper.

I opened the mirrored closet to see three hanging shirts and a second suit. There was a black suitcase on the stand.

The last door led to the bathroom.

The far end table contained the Gideon Bible, the telephone book, and the hotel guest services directory.

There were six drawers in the bureau, all empty except for the top right one which contained three pairs each of socks and underwear. The man sure traveled light.

The near end table contained a personal alarm clock, an area guidebook, a car rental agreement dated yesterday afternoon, and the ticket for a nonstop return flight two days hence. It appeared Wodehouse was a Midwesterner.

After glancing at my watch, I went to the closet and started searching the suitcase. There was nothing inside or within any of the zippered compartments. Who didn't have stubs or receipts or loose cough drops floating around in their luggage?

I entered the bathroom.

Dirty towels were crumpled on the toilet, the floor, and the counter, an amazing number of towels for one guy.

In a perfectly neat row sat an electric razor, toothbrush, toothpaste, and aftershave. Wodehouse used the hotel soap and shampoo rather than bring his own.

The trashcan was empty except for the plastic bag.

After checking my watch, I started the shower.

Then I returned to the living room.

My time was my own until eleven o'clock, and then I could stay as long as I dared.

There was a knock at the door, two minutes early.

After taking off the gloves, I opened the door and moved aside so the waiter could roll in the wheeled table, glad to note that the running shower was easily heard from here.

"Where would you like this?"

"Right there is just fine."

He raised the bottle of scotch so that I could see the label, lifted the metal lid off both plates as if to prove he wasn't leaving me two orders of waffles.

"Looks great."

"Call if you need any coffee."

"What about scotch?"

He laughed. "I'd have to charge you for that." He handed me a leather folder with the slip and a hotel pen. I held the folder by the thin outside edges and suspected the pen wouldn't last the morning.

"Money's no object." I wrote in a twenty-five percent tip, approximated the signature I'd seen on the car rental agreement. "I couldn't afford to keep my job if it didn't come with an unquestioned expense account."

"Thank you, Mister Wodehouse." The room service waiter backed out of the room, smiling. "Just leave everything outside your door when you're done."

"You bet."

I put the gloves back on and then confirmed that the DO NOT DISTURB sign was still hanging from the doorknob.

After grabbing the pot of coffee, I headed for the bathroom to turn off the shower. I retrieved the hangered shirts, crumpled them into a ball, stoppered the sink, and placed them inside. Then I emptied the coffee pot over the wrinkled mess, the hot liquid reaching the overfill drain, just enough.

I wouldn't need to order another pot after all.

Back in the living room, I opened the scotch and tipped my head back, letting the molten nectar burn a path home.

With my free hand I hefted one egg at a time and hurled it at each wall in turn. The last egg was slightly overdone leading to a less-than-spectacular splatter.

I took another drag and placed the bottle on the center of the desk. What, no coasters?

The steaks were warmer than the eggs so I concentrated on the hash brown potatoes, scanning the room for an adequate application. "One potato, two potato, three potato, four."

Nothing sparked for me.

I went into the bedroom, spun a slow circle. Nothing came to me here either.

After scooping the two orders of hash browns into one of the metal lids, I went into the only room left and tipped the contents into the toilet. Then I tossed in a small dirty towel and used the plunger to stuff the mixture in.

Should I flush before I left, or would that mean Wodehouse would lose the opportunity to discover my visit? Yes, I'd skip the flood and give Wodehouse the satisfaction of disbelief.

The steak had cooled enough for me to pick one up and I bit off chunks as I paced the room looking for ideas.

The hotel would sue Wodehouse for damages, and he'd come after them for their lack of security. Actually, I was doing the guy a favor, spicing up his bland life with a story he'd tell until the day he died.

"Five potato, six potato, seven potato, more."

I paused for another sip of scotch. Then I resumed my thinking and my steak.

It was a nice piece of meat, cooked just the way I liked

it, tender on the inside and slightly crispy on the outside.

What was I going to do with the toast?

I'd eat one slice, which left me with almost half-a-dozen. Even the thought of globbing on jelly first didn't spawn any sudden creative burst.

There was no point rushing genius. The toast would wait.

I tore open the sugar packets and poured the white powder through the vents atop both televisions.

While I was in the bedroom, I noticed the time and couldn't believe my eyes. I had to start making calls in five minutes.

I laid the second steak in the middle of the living room carpet and sat at the desk with my piece of toast.

At exactly eleven o'clock, I dialed the first number.

"Simons and Brown."

"I hope I'm not disturbing you."

"Excuse me?"

"My name is Fred Wassermann. I've been calling Brown every day for two weeks now." I swung my legs up onto the desk.

"He's been very busy."

"I'm happy for him. Meanwhile, my ex-wife has taken off with my kid. Brown was supposed to get me custody to keep that from happening."

"I'll let him know you're expecting his call."

"You or one of your clones has said that each time I've tried to talk with him. Are you sure Brown still works for your firm? Maybe he retired."

"Perhaps you'd like to speak to Mr. Simons."

"Do you think he's capable of tracking down my ex-wife and bringing back my kid? He doesn't have to slap her around or anything, just get my son for me."

There was a slight pause before the transfer went through.

"Mr. Simons."

"There's something I forgot to tell your secretary. I planted a bomb in your office. You have five minutes."

I disconnected and wiped toast crumbs from my shirt.

One down, three to go.

"Commonwealth Financial."

"This is David Wanker from across the street, and I can see black smoke pouring out of your building."

"Are you sure?"

"It's kind of hard to miss. Have you called 911 yet?"

"Bye ..."

I took a sip of scotch and rolled it around on my tongue as I dialed the next number.

"United Gas and Power."

"Hey, this is Joe over at Washington and Main. We got a bad leak here, and I'm afraid it could blow. We probably want to evacuate the whole freakin' block, and I need some extra hands if I'm going to keep this thing from knocking down half the city."

"Are police on the scene yet?"

"Nobody here but a bunch of rubberneckers hoping to meet their maker."

"I'm dispatching three crews and will contact police and fire."

"Thanks. Pray for me."

It was a good thing I hadn't had any ideas for the toast, because I was still really hungry. I snagged two more pieces and nearly swallowed one whole before I called the final number.

"Yes?"
"Done."

I stood and stretched.

Thirteen minutes remained until my next series of calls.

The unused toast was still nagging at me. I could grind it up into crumbs and then ... what?

I giggled as the image of crumbs sideslipped into something else. After retrieving a towel from the bathroom, I wrapped it around the two glasses. Then I slammed the package against an inside wall a couple dozen times.

In the bedroom, I carefully unfolded the towel on the bureau. Then I used a room service spoon to slide glass fragments into each of Wodehouse's socks, which I carefully refolded and replaced in their original position in the drawer.

What were the odds he'd check his socks before pulling them on tomorrow morning?

I shook out the remaining glass shreds in the shower, turned on the water and watched them sparkle their way down the drain. The towel went onto the floor with the other dirty laundry.

Thirsty, I went back to the bottle of scotch.

I took another slug to loosen my imagination. That toast was really bothering me. The word *country* aside, it was nothing more than warmed bread. How could I be defeated by bread?

"A man can't live on bread alone. The best thing since sliced bread. Bread is slang for money. Okay, toast then. Toast always lands buttered side down. He was toast."

Lifting a lamp, I hurled it at the coffee table, but the cord came up short, so it landed on the couch. Frankly, I wasn't in the mood. I picked up the desk chair and smashed the lamp to smithereens.

I tossed the chair aside to catch my breath. I didn't want to be panting when ... I glanced at my watch and swore. I was two minutes late.

The toast was going to be the death of me.

My fingers were shaking as I dialed the first number, which rang and rang. *Hurry up and answer the phone.*

"Truesdale Elementary School."

"Hi, I'm calling from the parking lot. I just saw some kids slip into the building with rifles."

"Oh, my god."

"You had better call the police."

Late, I was late.

"One Price Dry Cleaning."

"What?"

"One Price Dry Cleaning."

"Shit, I must have misdialed."

I took a deep breath, counted to two, splashed some scotch down my throat.

"Speedy Towing."

"There's got to be a fifteen-car pileup off the highway ramp, wrecked vehicles all over the damn place."

"Thanks for the tip."

My dialing finger hovered over the buttons. I couldn't remember the next number. There was a double digit. *Think, damn it, think. Oh yes.*

"911. Your call is being recorded."

"There's a jumper on top of the bank. I can see him from my window ..." I broke the connection. The cops would know I called from the hotel, but there were at least five banks visible from here.

Now the only question was whether or not my tardiness would cause any problems. All that planning, and I was two minutes late on my end. He'd waste me if he was caught because I blew the timetable.

I fortified myself with another belt of scotch before dialing the final number.

"Yes?"

"It's me. How did it go?" I closed my eyes.

"Smooth as silk."

"Clean getaway?"

"Free and clear."

I nearly whooped with relief. "How much did we get?"

"Thirty-seven dollars. The clerk tried to hold out on me but I could see the roll of quarters from where I was standing."

"Were there cameras?"

"Doesn't matter. The store had three cans of lighter fluid on the shelves so I torched the place. We don't need to worry about the clerk describing me either."

"Good deal. I'll meet you at the parking garage."

"In thirty?"

"Better make it forty-five. There's a complication."

"Need help?"

"Nah. I can take care of it, no problem."

"Forty-five then."

I hung up and raised the bottle of scotch in celebration before taking another swig. Then I sighed, wiping my mouth with the back of my arm. It was a little early yet to celebrate.

What the fuck was I going to do with that toast?

A Dog Named Mule

Wishbone Lane was a dead-end road, the last property a restored farmhouse used to rehabilitate kennel dogs. I wasn't here for the dogs. I was here to determine if Sheridan also distributed the heroin that killed my client's daughter.

I stopped my car.

Along the right of the drive was a fenced-in paddock containing a scaled-down obstacle course. There were jumps and moats, ramps and seesaws, all manner and size of open tubing.

A middle-aged man watched me from the center, a black lab by his side.

Walking over to the fence, I called out, "Sheridan?"

"That's me. And this is Mule. He's the most stubborn dog I've ever seen." Sheridan scooped up the dog in both arms and set him down astride a moat.

The dog stiffened.

Shaking his head, Sheridan came to meet me. "I think I could leave the dog there overnight and find him in the same exact position tomorrow morning."

"Perhaps he has vampire in his blood and he can't cross moving water."

Sheridan huffed. "Just plain stubborn. He doesn't even come when I call the dogs to dinner, just takes his own sweet time. So what can I do for you?"

"What's with the miniature jumps?"

"Agility training. I teach the dogs to run the course. It's excellent exercise, builds their confidence and trust, gets their brain working again after the kennel and whatever came before."

"What's Mule's story?"

Sheridan turned to look at the dog. "I don't know. Animal Control picked him up as a stray. No signs of abuse, but he'd been on his own for a while."

"How did he end up here?"

"After ten days in the kennel without being claimed by the current owner, the Animal Control Officer brings them to me. I'm the local dog psychologist slash physical therapist. Dogs that have been here to the ranch have a one hundred percent adoption rate."

"What about straight kennel dogs?"

"You don't want to know." Sheridan held my gaze. "So, you represent some charitable foundation looking to spread the wealth?"

"I heard about this place, thought I'd check it out."

"You a reporter?"

"The name's Harold Brodsky."

Sheridan smiled. "That still doesn't tell me what you do."

I glanced around. "Nice piece of land you have here."

"If you're in real estate, I'm not interested in selling."

"You'd be crazy to give up this location."

"You aren't a cop."

"We should all be so lucky to have a union contract with guaranteed pay increases."

Sheridan grinned. "So you're private."

"That's what my friends tell me."

Nodding, Sheridan turned to face the street. "I wonder

which of them complained." He turned back. "See here. I'm fully licensed through the Town Clerk's Office. I've got Health Department approval and a letter from the Zoning Board."

"You also have a file on the second floor of the police station."

"Empty."

I shook my head. "Thin. There's a difference."

"First I bump heads with Mule. Then you show up."

"I'm investigating allegations."

"People can't wait to smear someone doing good."

My nod took in the property. "You have an expensive hobby."

"People make donations, the occasional charitable foundation. It's tough to compete with the big guys but I get by. You're speaking to the President and Chair of No Bad Dogs, a charitable nonprofit corporation."

"You sound like a very important man. I apologize for not calling ahead to make an appointment. Do you get many visitors?"

"Tom Rice, you probably passed him sitting on his porch, he'll remember you as my first company all week. Tom isn't nosy, just likes to sit outside."

"How do you adopt out the dogs if no one comes here?"

"I don't. That's handled at the kennel. Every two weeks the Animal Control Officer brings out a load of new dogs, picks up the rehabilitated ones." Sheridan paused. "Just what are you trying to get at with your questions? You're digging a lot of holes, but I don't see it amounting to much."

"Six weeks ago, a college student died from an

overdose."

"I read about that, very sad."

"Some people say you supply the dealer on campus."

Sheridan laughed. "You might have noticed I'm in the dog business. Honestly, do I look like a drug dealer? You see any porn stars draped on my arms, goons hanging from the trees? I have a four-year-old pickup truck in the garage, and half the time, I smell like dog."

"Someone will talk. They always do."

Sheridan turned back towards Mule. The dog was still standing in the same exact spot. "Maybe you need a little grounding to clear your head of all the crazy talk you've been hearing. How about once Mule is back in shape, I have the kennel hold him for you."

"Are you offering me a dog?"

"You'd still have to pay the kennel fees, reimburse them for any medical expenses. In Mule's case, that wouldn't amount to much more than shots."

"You think the company of a good dog would help set me straight."

His eyes twinkled. "It couldn't hurt."

"Thanks, but I'll pass."

"If you're worried about the cost, I buy food in bulk at a deep discount. I could pass along the savings. Or if you want to buy your own, I could give you the money instead."

And Bingo was his name-o. The courts didn't recognize attempted bribery as a confession, but it was near enough for me. "How much are we talking about?"

"Depends on how many dogs you want to adopt."

"Say I adopted six."

"Then you'd need a kennel license. It's a town by-law."

Sheridan was smooth. If Detective Underhill hadn't pointed me in this direction, I never would have suspected the man standing before me. "How many dogs can I have without one?"

"Three."

"So say I adopted three."

"Three dogs, food for a year. Visits to the vet, squeaky toys. Be about ten grand."

"What if I just took Mule?"

"He's a good eater. He might cost you ten grand all by himself."

Mule still hadn't moved a muscle. "I wouldn't have to worry about spending money on a leash."

"Don't kid yourself. The next time you see Mule, you'll think he's a different dog."

Deciding I wasn't going to get anything else today, I let him know I wasn't folding. "Don't kid yourself. The next time I see Mule will probably be tomorrow when I come back to investigate further."

Sheridan didn't even blink. "You'll make Tom Rice's day."

I let Sheridan have the last word and returned to my car. He'd make a mistake, or he wouldn't. Meanwhile, I'd pressure the alleged dealer on campus.

Lewis lived on the second floor of a house about two blocks from the college. He sold drugs to pay rent and tuition, support his own addiction to betting big on college sports.

The first thing I noticed when Lewis let me in were the dog toys. They were everywhere. Then I saw the largest television I'd ever seen.

"So what was it you wanted to talk to me about?"

"I'm investigating the conditions in off-campus housing. Are you happy here?"

He shrugged. "It suits me."

"They allow pets?"

"I pay extra every month, had to put down a larger deposit than usual."

"Any problems with bugs?"

"No, nothing like that." He dropped into a recliner, nodded towards the couch. "Take a load off."

"Thanks." I wished that television was on so I could see what kind of picture he got. "How are the neighbors?"

"More quiet than I'd find in a dorm. The guy in the house next door, he's got these floodlights he turns on after dark. I swear, some nights it's so bright in my bedroom, I could probably study."

"Must drive your dog crazy."

"Actually, I'm between dogs right now."

"I'm sorry."

"Oh, Rusty didn't die. He jumped ship, literally. By the time I righted the canoe he had swum to shore and took off into the woods after whatever he saw in the first place. He never came back."

"That surprises me."

"I've put up flyers, left word with the pound. What else can I do?"

"Is there any other reason you'd choose off-campus versus on-campus housing?"

Lewis took a moment to think. "It's easier to park, that's for sure. You have any other questions?"

I stood. "Not right now. There may be some follow-up later."

Lewis shook my extended hand. "Perhaps the school

can pressure the landlords to keep rent down."

"I'll pass along your suggestion."

As Lewis shut the door behind me, I promised myself I'd be back, if only to see that television in action.

I took note of the red Ford Explorer in the driveway. Lewis obviously didn't believe in a low profile. Perhaps he used gambling to explain his purchases.

Then it was back to Campus Security. There was no drug problem at the school. They regretted the recent tragedy, but she must have brought the illegal substance back with her after a visit home.

I left academia behind to re-enter the real world. Then I changed my mind and swung by the station, which was its own kind of cloistered environment.

"Well, if it isn't Harold Brodsky."

"How come whenever I stop by the second floor, day or night, here you are?" I pulled a chair closer to his desk so I could rest my feet on the edge.

Detective Underhill knocked them off. "That's because I'm a dedicated professional."

"No, why aren't you out on the street solving crimes? They could pay a baboon to sit behind your desk."

"He's already busy in the Chief's office."

I laughed.

"So what brings you in? Hoping I'll take you to lunch?"

"Why make such a big deal about it? You'll put it on your expense report, call me an informant ..."

He held up his hand. "Improving liaison relations. LR is very big right now."

"And then you'll get reimbursed."

"In six months at the earliest. The Chief got all new furniture, again, and the department floats into the next fiscal year on what they owe me. But you don't want to hear about my problems."

"No, I do. My life sounds so much better in comparison."

Underhill grinned. "Why don't you take me out to lunch then. You can always bill it to your next client."

"Speaking of helping me ..."

He blinked. "I don't remember using those words."

"I was wondering if you'd made any headway."

"On which of my fourteen open cases?"

"Denise Elkin."

Underhill tipped his chair back, rested his head against the wall. "As soon as I recommended you to the family, I wrote that one off as solved."

"Thanks for the vote of confidence, but I was hoping for something more tangible."

"There's nothing new at this end." He brought his chair back to the floor, leaned on the desk. "When we weren't even able to catch Sheridan and Lewis together, the investigation was quietly squelched. We aren't welcome on school property. It upsets the ostriches."

"Lewis lives on private property."

Underhill shook his head. "Actually, that house is owned by the school. Most of the off-campus housing is. They bought the two nearest convenience stores, not to mention three liquor stores and the four pizza places that deliver. Education is big business. My hands are tied."

I shrugged as I stood. "In that case, I'll be too busy solving this on my own to take you to lunch. Maybe next time."

"Just keep me informed."

Since Lewis was the most likely to break, as he could

cut a deal in exchange for Sheridan, I drove back to his apartment and parked across the street.

I knew Underhill wasn't as disinterested as he pretended. Being a cop, he was forced to work within a system that didn't always revolve around justice. He picked the fights he thought he could win, and then the department tied one hand behind his back. Sometimes it was both of them.

A young woman wearing a backpack approached the house. When she turned up the walkway to the first floor apartment, I dashed across the street before she finished unlocking the door.

"Excuse me, Miss."

She tensed, spread her keys between her fingers in the classic defense. "Yes?"

I repeated the story I'd told Lewis. "You're the last person I need to talk to today. Sorry if I startled you, but I'm looking forward to getting home."

"What do you want to know?"

Apparently, we were talking on the front steps. At least she hadn't run or screamed for the police. "I was upstairs earlier. You must find it noisy living under a dog owner."

"I've never known anyone who had such bad luck with pets."

"What do you mean?"

"Lewis. Every other week he has a new dog."

"That seems odd."

"I asked him about it once. He said he can't bear to use a leash, and the dogs keep running off, maybe to search for their previous owner."

"Previous owner?"

"Lewis adopts dogs from the shelter." She finally

smiled. "You know, typical college student, trying to do the right thing."

"That's nice of him." I directed the conversation back to the supposed purpose of my visit, asked her the same questions I'd posed to Lewis earlier, quickly wrapped it up.

Back in my car, I drove to the nearest parking lot and called Underhill. "Remember how you said you couldn't prove Sheridan and Lewis ever met? I think I know how Sheridan is passing the drugs."

"Tell me I can set up a surveillance. Tell me it's not on school property."

"Even better. Would you believe town property? Heck, it probably even falls under the jurisdiction of the police department."

"You just couldn't give me good news without following it with bad." He sighed. "Fire away."

"It's the dog pound. Sheridan is using the strays that he supposedly rehabilitates at his place. Lewis adopts a new dog on a weekly basis."

"I don't suppose there's any chance that no one from Animal Control is involved."

"Nobody legit would let the same person adopt that many dogs. Besides, the pound is where money changes hands." I recalled Sheridan's description of the process. "Anyone else who happens to be in the office at the time is probably told the large sum is a donation or to cover medical expenses."

"If there's any silver lining, we shouldn't need a search warrant. Heck, they store their old records in our basement."

"Do you know the Animal Control Officer?"

"Not well enough to vouch for him. He'd certainly have an easier time hiding the inconsistencies than someone on his staff would. The Chief is going to go nuts."

"How soon can you set up the surveillance? I don't know how often the transfer happens, but Lewis is between dogs."

"My people would be recognized. We work too closely with the Animal Control folks. Since it's your case, why don't you be the one to set up camp? Just let me know when Lewis shows up. If I don't hear from you by next week, I'll have a patrol car drop you off some sandwiches."

"That's thoughtful of you."

I spent the next two days parked down the street from the pound. On the morning of the third day I saw a red Ford Explorer approach.

When the vehicle pulled into the lot, I called Underhill.

"Wait for us."

"It depends how long you take."

Lewis had been inside for five minutes when I saw him leave the pound with a dog that strained at the leash, a dog that just might have been Mule. Sheridan was right. I almost didn't recognize him.

The dog certainly wasn't standing still now.

I pulled in behind the Explorer when Lewis passed.

There was no sign of Underhill.

Lewis drove the speed limit, obeyed all the traffic laws. Apparently he thought he knew the difference between flashy and stupid.

We were getting close to college property and I still didn't see Underhill in my mirror.

At the next stoplight, I tapped Lewis's rear end.

He came out of the Explorer yelling but stopped when

he recognized me. "You."

I stepped out of my car and closed the distance.

"Glad to see you finally got another dog."

"What is this? You hit my car." He turned away to examine his bumper.

I walked up to the window. "Mule."

Lewis looked up. "What?"

"You adopted Mule. I met him out at Sheridan's."

"I don't know any Sheridan." He shook his head at whatever damage he saw back there. "I don't care what the insurance company says. You're paying my deductible."

Mule was pacing the backseat frantically. All of a sudden, he squatted. "Your dog is doing his business in the car."

As Lewis ran around to the door on the other side, I saw the condom of white powder poking out from the dog's stool.

That's when Underhill and a cruiser joined us.

I smiled at Lewis through the windows. "Unless you want to spend more time in prison than necessary, I'd suggest you try to remember Sheridan. In detail."

Though my client of course didn't get his daughter back, he did get to see some justice. Sheridan, Lewis, and the Animal Control Officer were all sentenced to prison time.

My good friend Detective Underhill was able to close a case and thumb his nose at the political hacks at the same time.

Me, once the check cleared, I spent two weeks pricing large screen televisions. I settled on a new printer.

Fill It with the Cheapest

It started as a dare, and I'd give anything to be able to turn back the clock and swallow the words: "Bet you can't."

"Oh, are you challenging me?" Sandra shot me a look that said she'd already accepted and doubled the stakes. "You just rest your weary head, old man, and I'll wake you at the first breakfast place I see after the sun rises."

"You don't want to drive through the night."

"I can, and I do. Maybe I'm no longer the college sophomore you unwittingly seduced, but that doesn't mean I can't still handle an all-nighter."

Staying up to cram for an exam and then crashing was one thing. Driving a car on unlighted, unfamiliar roads was another. "The thing is, I could use a shower. Maybe you should stop at the first motel."

"Nice try. I've put up with your stink this long, another day won't make a difference."

"Okay, then." I'd slept badly the night before, and work today was brutal. I simply didn't have the energy to argue.

This was our first vacation in three years. Our schedules finally meshed, and Sandra suggested we drive back and visit the bed and breakfast where we'd married. It would be romantic.

"Wouldn't seeing an away game be romantic?"

End of discussion.

Sandra called the B&B to make reservations, tracked down directions. I gassed up her car, checked the oil, and topped off the coolant.

"Before you fall asleep and leave me here driving all alone, could you find a good radio station?"

"Sure." I reached for the tuner. "Talk or music?"

"Music."

"Hard or soft?"

"Soft."

"Adult contemporary or instrumental?"

"Instrumental."

"Classical or jazz?"

"Classical."

"Symphony or chamber?"

"Wait! Stop there."

I froze. "That's polka."

"Yes. Isn't it fun?"

I sat back in my seat and closed my eyes. Polka was not fun. As far as I was concerned, it didn't even count as music.

Sandra slapped my leg. "The driver picks the station."

"I didn't say anything."

"Heaven forbid."

That polka ended, and one that sounded exactly identical began. I fell asleep in self-defense.

"Fill it with the cheapest."

I forced an eye open and winced at the bright fluorescent lighting of an overnight gas station.

Sandra was tapping the wheel in time to a polka.

I grunted but fell back asleep before finishing the thought.

I was dreaming I was a goldfish, swimming around my bowl, darting in and out of the sunken pirate ship, the haunted castle, the plastic plants and coral. That's when someone knocked on the window and woke me up.

She smiled. "We'll be open in ten minutes."

"Okay." I shook my head, but it didn't help. Sandra was gone, but I could see her purse sticking out from under the seat, so she didn't go far. Surprised she didn't wake me.

I fumbled my door open and staggered out onto the concrete, stretched and shook my whole body, spat.

If Sandra didn't go far, she didn't go anywhere. The gas station was the only building in sight.

Smacking my lips, I walked over to the office where I could see my morning angel straightening shelves. I pushed the door, but it didn't move. Apparently, the ten minutes weren't up.

Right above my hand were the hours. Monday through Saturday, 7:00 a.m. to 9:00 p.m. Sunday, 7:00 a.m. to 9:00 p.m.

This must not have been where we stopped last night.

I walked back to the car to see if Sandra was asleep on the back seat. She wasn't. Keys were in the ignition.

Behind me, I heard the office door being unlocked.

I wandered over.

The door opened when I pushed, and I picked up a bag of chips before going to the counter and smiling back at the woman who woke me. The name "Betty" was stitched over her left breast.

"Sorry about sleeping out at your pumps."

"No harm done."

"Do you happen to know if there's a restaurant nearby?"

"There's the Crazy Loon, but they don't serve breakfast."

I raised the chips. "Breakfast is taken care of. No, I'm

looking for a small function room."

"You want to hold a meeting or something?"

"Actually I'm scouting for a private wedding ceremony. Just me, the bride, and someone to do the paperwork."

"Congratulations." She beamed. "The Loon has a small room you could probably use. It's nice."

"Thanks for the tip."

She nodded. "Are you going to get gas or just the chips?"

"Just the chips for now." I handed her a five.

Betty gave me my change. "Don't mind my asking, but how did you choose here to get married?"

"Randomly."

I went outside and found a large, flat rock to sit on. Then I opened the bag of chips and started eating.

Not a car went by.

It was no wonder the Crazy Loon didn't serve breakfast. If this was the beginning of rush hour traffic, it was amazing that the Crazy Loon stayed in business at all.

My car blocking one of the pumps was obviously not going to be a problem for the gas station. I wondered what Betty was doing inside, how she entertained herself to pass the hours.

Was she reading a tabloid or completing a crossword puzzle? Was she singing along with the radio or writing poetry? Was she painting her fingernails or watching the handsome stranger eat his breakfast?

I crumpled the empty bag and stuffed it into my left pocket.

How did a town like this survive? Why did anybody ever stay? If it was me that was born here, I'd grab the first ride out and never look back. Hit the highway without so much as a fare-thee-well.

"Are you okay?"

I turned to see Betty standing a few feet away. "Sure. That's kind of you to ask."

She had large, trusting eyes. "Is something wrong with your car? I can call Bob to come in. He's a mechanic."

"No, I'm just tired. I drove all night, and I'm afraid I'll fall asleep at the wheel if I drive any further."

"Where are you going?"

"Only about another twenty miles. But I'm just spent."

"I could drive you."

"Really?"

She nodded. "We don't get much business before noon. No one would even know I was gone."

"That would be great." I stood and dusted off my pants. "I'll even pay you for your time. Then you can add 'professional chauffeur' to the list of your work experiences."

Betty laughed. "I just need to put a sign on the door to say when I'll be back."

"You do that."

I returned to the car, squirmed until I found a comfortable position, fell asleep.

The sound of Betty closing her door woke me. "You weren't kidding when you said you were tired."

"No."

Betty started the car. "But if you're not awake, how can you give me directions?"

"Nudge me when we reach the town line."

I heard her say: "If I'm going to be a chauffeur, I should really have a hat." Then I went out again.

I was dreaming I was a bird flying tight loops within a

padded cage, the tip of both wings brushing against the rubbery substance that encased the bars for my own protection.

"We're here at the end of incorporated property."

Rubbing my eyes, I sat up. "Hit the gas."

Betty giggled. "That's the sum of your directions?"

"Have you ever left town before?"

"I think maybe once. My eighth grade science class was hiking through the woods and we may have passed the borders. I'm not certain but we walked for an awful long time."

"Push the pedal to the metal."

Betty accelerated, looked at me with naked glee in her eyes. "So where are we going?"

"Where would you like to go?"

"Vegas."

"Vegas it is. Wake me when it's time for me to tell you to take a left."

I was dreaming I was a lone wolf, rogue of the pack, with gray hair that bristled in the moonlight. All of my legs were stuck in a rusted trap, and no matter how much I gnawed, I couldn't bite myself free.

Betty tapped me on the shoulder. "Let's go in for a drink."

Night had fallen, and I shaded my eyes from the neon glare as we crossed the parking lot, Betty with one hand in my back pocket.

"Did you drive all day without a break?"

"Once I started moving, I just couldn't stop."

"You're living an adventure."

"Thanks to you."

Betty led me over to the bar where we climbed onto

two empty stools. She placed a twenty on the imitation mahogany. I placed my head next to the bill.

Fade to black.

"Fill it with the cheapest."

I pried my eyes open far enough to see Betty pointing at her empty mug.

My lids slammed shut.

I was dreaming in black and white. There was no sound. The images were hypnotic, flowing past me like an icy stream that cascades over polished stones.

"Last call. You want another drink?"

I sat up, coughed. There was an empty mug in front of the stool to my left, a wrinkled twenty.

I blinked at the bartender. She wore a white shirt with a black bow tie, her sleeves unbuttoned but not rolled up.

"Do you have coffee?"

"Not yet. After we close."

I laid my head back down.

"Cream and sugar?"

I stirred, stretched. "Black will be fine."

"You want a shot of something?" The bow tie was gone and her shirt opened.

"I don't drink."

"What are you doing in a bar?"

We were the only two still here, a single lit light hanging over our heads. "I heard you served a mean cup of coffee."

"It will kick you when you're down, that's for sure."

"Is it true that bartenders hear everything: every conceivable story, every bold dream, every brazen lie?"

She shook her head. "There's usually too much background noise. I nod a lot. Half the time people probably don't even get the drink they ordered, but they can't tell or don't care."

"What's your name?"

"Charlene."

"You must be sick of being told you have a pretty name."

"No one has ever mentioned it."

"You're kidding."

"Yes, I am." She finished her coffee. "I need to lock up."

I stepped off the stool, lost my balance, grabbed the edge of the bar to keep myself from tumbling.

"Are you sure you don't drink?"

"I'm so tired, I feel drunk."

"Let me help you out to your car."

She swung my right arm around her neck and we turned off the light, locked the front door, and kicked an empty beer bottle off the walkway into the bushes.

"Dump me in the passenger seat. I'm in no shape to drive."

"Can I give you a lift somewhere? They'll tow your car if it stays here overnight, even if you're in it."

"What about your car?"

"I walk to work. Unless it's raining. Then I run."

"I appreciate your concern."

"Maybe if you come back, you'll order something and leave me a tip."

We opened the door and I slid inside.

I was dreaming in color, but everything was red, and I couldn't determine where one thing ended and another began.

"Where to?"

I cleared my throat and wiped the stickiness from my

eyes. "Just drive. You don't have to be up early, do you?"

"Not any more. Bartending was my mad money, but last week I got laid off at my real job. Twenty percent of the workforce was cut."

"That's tough." Her face glowed in the lights from the dashboard.

"I'm still too shocked to recognize the next step. Do I stay here and try to find another job? Move and start all over? Go back to school?"

I curled up as best I could. "Take your time."

Charlene sniffed. "No offense, but something stinks."

"Oh that. I need to empty the trunk."

A Friendly Game

Perini closed the folders on his desk as soon as he saw the shadow on the pebbled glass. The door opened, and Jack poked his head inside. "Have a minute?"

"Sure." Jack owned the manufacturing shop that filled ninety-seven percent of Building A, and the management company that ran the industrial park had been more than delighted when Perini Investigations offered to rent the virtually unusable remainder. "What's up?"

Jack stopped just inside the door. "I don't know if you know, but the shop has a softball team. There's a big game tonight, and we're short a player. You interested?"

"Me?" Perini chuckled. "I haven't played ball of any sort in years."

"Not a problem. You can hang out in right field. Probably won't even have to put down your beer. I'd really appreciate the favor."

"Sounds like fun."

"We'll stop in at quitting time with the details."

Perini watched the door swing closed behind his new team captain. Imagine that. As a cop, Perini had accepted being ostracized by society and his own growing us/them mentality because fellow officers provided a sense of community. As a private investigator, he had no one but himself.

He ate alone, and he drank alone, and he slept alone.

Even when he attended the occasional PI convention, he listened to the lectures and watched the demonstrations and tested the gadgets alone.

Compare that to Jack, who was not only married but worked with his wife, who ran a shop filled with employees, who apparently spent his off hours as part of a team. Heck, Jack might even have close friends.

Perini rubbed his face. There were no mean streets. Only mean lives.

"Take me out to the ball game."

He surprised himself with a smile before returning to his filing.

Ten minutes after five, Jack led Sheila through the front door. "We still on for tonight?"

"You bet." His wife looked everywhere but at Perini. If she was impressed with his efforts to organize the mess, she hid it well.

"Great." Jack flashed a thumbs-up. "We play over at Lopes Memorial. Need a glove?"

"I'm all set."

"The game starts at seven, but we practice at six-thirty."

"Six-thirty it is."

"See you then."

Perini waited for the door to close behind the couple before he locked up his papers and another five minutes before leaving his office. There was a sporting goods store over on Magri, where he would be able to buy a softball glove.

The parking lot was empty, and Perini whistled as he walked to his car.

Overall, the day had been good. He'd made some calls, tracked down facts that touched a dozen cases, and caught up on paperwork. Pretty soon he'd be standing out in right field, waiting for the crack that signaled a ball coming his way.

Perini fiddled with the radio as he drove, hoping to hear a game, but all he could find was music. That figured. He left the radio on a station playing soft jazz and thought about what else he might need.

Jack had mentioned beer but neglected to say whether it was provided or whether Perini should bring his own. Well, picking some up wasn't exactly an impossible task. Bring enough to share, make a few points, maybe a few friends. There was no reason this had to be a one-time event.

Maybe he should try to arrive early, learn the lay of the land.

Did he need cleats?

Perini laughed at himself, and it felt good.

He changed radio stations until he found a song he could hum.

By six-fifteen he was parked at Lopes Memorial, eating a microwaved sandwich and waiting for the others to arrive. In the back seat were three cases of beer: regular, lite, and imported. If he was going to play ball with these folks, it made sense to cover his bases.

Perini glanced at his dashboard clock again.

It was still early.

What if he stank? What if, instead of making the game-winning play, he missed every ball that flew his way and embarrassed himself at the plate? He'd never get invited back.

Two cars pulled into the lot. By the time the drivers climbed out and high-fived, three more cars had arrived.

Perini finished his sandwich and wiped his mouth with a paper napkin.

No one was carrying beer. No one was wearing cleats. The team uniform appeared to be jeans and a t-shirt. Perini would look odd out in right field wearing long sleeves.

The players gathered on the diamond. One stretched, and one did jumping jacks while the others talked.

Should Perini wait for Jack to arrive so he could introduce him? Just how often did Jack bring in a substitute?

The man himself drove into the lot, and the players converged on his car.

Perini took a deep breath before joining them.

The men were carrying mesh bags of equipment from Jack's trunk. Two cases of beer from a local brewery. Perini had missed that angle.

Jack slapped him on the shoulder. "Glad you could make it."

"Can't let the team down."

Jack laughed before making a series of rapid introductions. He paused. "Where are Gomez and Treat?"

"Here comes Gomez now."

The mesh bags were emptied of bats and balls while Jack handed out hats and numbered blue jerseys.

"I hope you don't mind 12."

Perini shrugged. "Fine with me."

"Don't worry. They're washed between games."

Noticing the others shucking their t-shirt before putting on their jersey, Perini did likewise. The clothes went on the first bleacher along with the beer. Cell phones went on the second one. Perini was glad he hadn't brought his gun.

Someone whooped.

"Looks like Treat decided to show up after all."

"Sorry guys."

"You know the rules."

Treat grabbed the plastic bases from one of the bags and ran the infield, dropping them in place. Everyone applauded as he completed the task.

Jack winked at Perini. "First home run of the game."

"Hope it's not the last."

Nodding, Jack pulled a whistle from his pocket and then blew twice. "Okay, listen up. We have fifteen minutes before the enemy—I mean the other team—comes begging for practice time. Let's look smart."

Perini jogged out to right field and then watched the infielders toss the ball around while the pitcher warmed up. Jack motioned the player on first towards the plate and each man in turn swung at a few pitches.

The shortstop hit a long fly ball, and Perini snagged it easily, his throw to first overshooting the raised glove. Well, that's what practice was for.

Perini stopped a second ball on a bounce, and then Jack waved him in for his chance at glory.

The bat was heavier than Perini expected. He swung twice as though he knew what he was doing and then assumed the position.

Two strikes were followed by a solid grounder to third.

Perini grinned.

More cars entered the parking lot and Jack checked his watch. "Two minutes."

The pace of the practice quickened as the focus changed to throwing and catching. Perini felt muscles that he'd forgotten slowly awaken and begin to perform as softballs passed from player to player, the effortless motion punctuated by satisfying smacks.

Jack blew two short bursts, and the team left the field for the bench.

"Looking good out there. Let's keep it up when it matters. Remember, the losing team staffs the volunteer table at the next blood drive, and the winners get to donate." He raised a hand. "More importantly, it's not whether you win or lose, but how badly you crush your opponent."

The team cheered and then watched their victims warm up.

The guy standing next to Perini, Treat, turned to face him. "You don't work for Jack, do you?"

"No, he just asked me to fill in."

"Cool. It's a good group of guys. We have fun."

Perini was glad Treat hadn't asked what he did for a living. He was finally part of a team again and didn't want to lose the feeling. "Everybody seems to be enjoying themselves."

Treat nodded. "Just don't commit any errors, or we'll have to take you behind the bleachers and beat the crap out of you."

"I'll keep that in mind. And what if I make the play that wins the game?"

"Jack kisses you full on the lips."

"Maybe I'll just let the ball roll through my legs."

The two men laughed.

Treat glanced at Perini's glove. "You play much softball?"

"Softball? I thought we were here to golf."

"Keep that up, and we'll vote you team captain."

Jack rushed onto the field pointing at his watch and

then waving his arms.

"That was quick." Perini checked the time.

"Oh, it's early. But the two captains will yell at each other until Jack apologizes for his watch running fast, and by then it will be seven and time to begin."

"Does he do this every game?"

The two captains stood with their faces only inches apart, screaming obscenities.

"No. Sometimes he fakes a heart attack."

Perini laughed so hard he had to fight to catch his breath. "You're joking."

"You can't find entertainment like this sitting at home watching the professionals."

Perini shook his head. "So what's up with number twelve, the guy I'm replacing? Did he have a heart attack, too?"

"Jack told him to call in sick today, do some fishing." Treat shrugged. "Management works in mysterious ways."

The two captains stopped yelling, and then both blew their whistles. Jack flipped a coin, watched for the opposing captain to call it, and then flashed a thumbs-up to his team before jogging over to their bench.

"We're up first. That will give us a chance to break their spirit by racking up a double-digit lead. I don't think their pitcher could find the strike zone if it was tattooed to his forehead. So let's make them wish they stayed home tonight and waxed the kitchen floor. Batting in position order."

Dolby stood and swung his arms as he walked to home plate.

Jack motioned Perini toward the bleachers.

"What's up?"

"I wanted to thank you for coming tonight."

"No problem. In fact ..."

Jack cut him off. "Sheila watches me like a hawk. Sometimes I think hiring her was the worst move I ever made. But that's beside the point. You do security work, right?"

Perini's microwaved sandwich felt like a baseball in his stomach. "There isn't much call for it."

"Good." Jack leaned away to shout at Dolby, "Raise your elbows." He rolled his eyes at Perini. "Sorry about that. Look, we don't have much time. I want to hire you to protect me."

"Has someone threatened you?"

"Not yet. I have a little something going on the side, but Sheila is getting suspicious. Tonight I'll tell her you were hopeless at softball, but we hit if off, and we're going to bowl on Sundays. Sheila hates bowling. All you have to do is back me up, talk to her on the phone once or twice to say you're running late. You know. I don't even care what you do on Sundays just so long as Sheila doesn't see you."

"You want me to be your alibi." The cement sent acid up Perini's throat. "That's why I'm here."

Jack leaned away again. "Go! Run to second, you lazy bum!" Jack shook his head. "Dolby could hit a ball out of the park and be satisfied with a single."

"Sorry, but it doesn't sound like the type of work I do."

"But I suppose you'd follow me if Sheila hired you, shoot telephoto pictures of the adulterous pair." Jack slapped Perini's shoulder. "Don't worry. I understand. Your job is your job. I respect a man with principles."

"I'm more of an investigator."

"And damn good, I'm sure. Hey, I tried. One of these

guys will cover for me. I just need to decide who's least likely to become a blackmailer." He snickered. "If you ever see one of these jokers wearing the title of Vice President, you'll know I guessed wrong."

"I should get back."

"No, stick around. We still need someone in right field."

Perini had meant back to the rest of the team. "Sure."

Last week, Jack's wife had floated the idea of Perini shadowing her husband.

Perini knew now that he would.

High Noon

Even though it was only quarter of, Patsy couldn't keep from going to the door again, standing on the threshold as her gaze tracked down the dirt driveway, down the open road that was empty as far as the eye could see. Feeling the slightest breeze, she stared down the gap of her open blue robe, small beads of sweat visible all the way down to her high-heeled shoes. It was only quarter of.

Patsy stepped back inside.

They'd rented the foreclosed farmhouse because Brad figured it made more sense to hide in the area rather than risk getting caught on the run. They'd been here three weeks now, waiting for the right moment, and Patsy didn't know how much longer she could stand it.

Patsy was a city girl. She was accustomed to sharp lights and dull noise, the vibrant decay of back alleys and the people who lived on the streets. Out here in the middle of nowhere, there wasn't even the scrambling of rats to remind her of home.

She splashed whiskey into a canning jar, set the bottle back on the butcher-block table, a table surrounded by tacky orange chairs. People had lived here. On purpose.

Patsy took a healthy slug of her drink.

Today was payday for the area's two largest employers, and the bank should be bursting with cash until lunch, when the hayseeds poured in waving their checks. Brad and she had watched the circus several times before they decided the target was too good to pass up.

They went back to the city to hire a driver and second gun, brought Steve and Michael back to live in the house these three long weeks.

Patsy had burned meals for the four of them and tried to divert the men from their boredom. Perhaps she had tried too hard. Booze was cheap out here and the days long.

Running a hand through her long blonde hair, Patsy glanced through the kitchen doorway to the front hall.

It was ten minutes of.

She scraped a chair out from under the table and sat, her elbows bracketing her drink. Now she was the one going out of her mind with boredom.

While she could have driven the car or handled the second gun, Brad didn't want their signature on the job. This bank was going to net them more than all the rest of their heists put together, and he didn't want the FBI to turn up the heat and start making connections.

Patsy shooed a fly from the canning jar.

When it was finally safe for them to leave this house, they'd take a right onto Easy Street and follow that boulevard to the end of the world. They'd be done with the nickel and dime jobs, done with scraping by.

Brad said he'd already lined up better living accommodations for them. Living accommodations. Patsy sniffed. Brad was already even talking fancier.

Patsy wiped away the sweat that was gathering on her inner thighs. She'd never enter a room again that wasn't air-conditioned. No, she had waited too long for the high life, listened to too many stories, watched too many dreams go bust.

Brad had thought he could pull off this job alone, but she'd quickly set him straight. He was sure to mess up if he tried it himself, and she argued that he needed two people to fill her shoes.

For once, he listened.

It was five minutes of.

Patsy sighed and took another slug of booze, wondering who and how many would come through the door.

The four of them had lived like farmers here, stinking in their own sweat, swatting at flies, following the weather like it was a matter of life or death.

She'd told Brad that they needed to hit the bank on a day when it rained in the morning. That way they wouldn't leave a trail of rising dust pointing straight at the house. She never thought rain would be so hard to come by.

The three men were restless. They missed the city, the action, the broads.

She slept with Steve while Brad and Michael were out back trying to bang together a shooting range. She slept with Michael while Steve practiced and Brad went into town to buy more whiskey. After those first times, arranging opportunities was both easier and harder.

Brad looked at her a little funny sometimes, but he must have known better than to complain. She was keeping his employees from raising hell.

Besides, the arrangement was only until they were blessed with a morning rain on payday. After the job, the men's lust would be fed by memories of the job and the piles of cash. Then Steve and Michael would split with their share.

At least, that's what Brad believed.

Two minutes of.

Patsy had kept herself from going crazy by improving on the original plan. Michael would shoot Brad while they were still in the bank and tell Steve a guard got lucky. Steve would wait until Michael loaded the money into the car and then shoot him and return to Patsy alone.

Steve had the potential to be a winner. Patsy could tell.

She'd been with Brad for enough years to know he'd find some way to turn this haul into just another in an endless series of robberies. He enjoyed the life too much.

Steve, on the other hand, simply sat in a car and drove. A rich man could do that in style.

As the clock chimed twelve, Patsy returned to the front door where she made certain the blue robe parted just enough.

Once they were back in the city, air conditioned, she'd do herself up right, show Steve what she was capable of.

Patsy looked down the driveway, down the empty road.

She squinted in the harsh sunlight, swatted at flies.

By one o'clock, when the radio confirmed the job had gone down, Patsy realized the boys had cut her loose.

She closed the robe and poured herself another drink.

Inn

Makeda entered the lobby, stamped the snow off her sneakers, and blew into her cupped hands, wincing when she saw how her honey-colored skin had cracked from the cold. She approached the white man behind the counter. "I'd like a room."

"I'm sorry, but we're full up. This sudden storm. I think half the people traveling the interstate today pulled off here rather than risk the weather."

"The sign outside says you have vacancies."

"I must have forgotten to throw the switch." He reached under the counter. "There. Now it doesn't."

"I've been on the road so long that I can't see straight." It was hard to know sometimes when something was racial. Strick always overreacted and then took out his frustrations on her. He didn't see anything wrong with that because they had the same color skin. That made it all right.

The clerk sniffed. "Even if you had reservations, there still wouldn't be a room available."

"Where's the nearest hotel?"

"Northbound, maybe ten exits. I don't know how long it would take, though. How's the driving?"

"It's bad." Makeda had never driven in snow before, which made her wonder about all the people she had seen spin out of control. Had they never seen it before either?

"Can you call, ask if there are any rooms left, before I head on over?"

"I don't know the name or even what town it's in." He shrugged. "I don't get out much since I lost my car."

"So what do you suggest I do?"

"You have any friends in this area, family?"

Not knowing anyone was the reason she'd chosen this direction. Stay away from everything she knew, and she'd be harder to track. At least, that was the theory. She was also banking on the idea that the cops wouldn't get too riled up about another dead black man. "My people aren't from around here."

"I don't know what to tell you then."

"Do you have a couch I can use? I'll pay. Cash."

He licked his teeth. "I wish I could help you, but it's against policy. I'd be fired."

"Don't tell anyone. I'll still pay. It doesn't even have to be with money." There came a time when no price was too high. Years with Strick had separated Makeda from her body, and she was too exhausted to care one way or another so long as she could sleep when it was over. There was nothing this man could take from her that hadn't already been stolen.

"I can't afford to lose this job."

"I understand." Instead of the relief she half expected, she felt her gut twist from the weight of disappointment. Why did nothing ever break her way? Why did everything always have to be so hard? "Can I borrow a piece of cardboard? Somebody threw a rock through my car window."

"I'll check out back. Wait here."

Makeda leaned against the counter. Except for gas, she

hadn't stopped since she left the apartment the day before last. Did she eat anything today? She couldn't remember.

Strick had controlled her for so long that she wasn't sure she still knew how to recognize when she was hungry. Tired, she knew. Tired was when her bones ached, when her eyes stung, when nothing but nothing mattered but the promise of escape. Tired was how she was now.

"Here you go." He handed her the top of a paper box.

"Thanks. That's great. I'll just rest some in the parking lot before I move on."

"I'm afraid that's not possible."

"Why?" If she let her eyes close, she'd fall asleep standing up.

"The police sweep through every hour looking for drug deals. They'd arrest you if they caught you in your car."

At least then she could sleep in a warm jail cell. But the incident would be a matter of public record, and then they'd find her without even having to look. She sighed. "I guess I'll be on my way. Thanks for the box."

"Good luck."

Makeda hunched her shoulders against the cold and hurried through the falling snow towards her car. She should have asked the clerk for some tape, since how else would she hold the cardboard in place?

First, get the heat going. Then she'd worry about trying to repair the window, the victim of another act of senseless violence, but then, weren't they all.

Nothing happened when she turned the key in the ignition.

Makeda counted to three and tried again. Again, at the count of two. Again. Now what?

She was sitting surrounded by vehicles. Someone had

to be willing to give her a jump. She couldn't let herself imagine that the car needed anything more.

After putting the keys in her coat pocket, she ran toward the building, glad for what little protection it offered, a hallway overhead that blocked the snow. She could see the NO VACANCY sign from here, shining beneath the neon WELCOME INN. The parking lot was full. The clerk probably hadn't been lying about there being nothing available.

He also said he didn't have a car, which meant she needed to find someone else to jump her.

Makeda stamped her feet on the concrete walk and then started toward the nearest room, where light shot through a crack between the curtains.

Please let it be a woman who answered the door.

Makeda knocked.

He wore dark pants, an undershirt, and a scowl that couldn't hide the mean. "I don't need turn-down."

"I don't work here. My car battery. I think it died."

He stared at her. "So?"

"Do you have jumper cables?"

His gaze slipped past her. "Why don't you wait inside. Close the door before any more snow blows in." He turned away and disappeared into the bathroom.

Makeda entered the small room and shivered, not from the cold. The place was a mess, dirty clothes lying where they'd landed, shrunken effigies of the man who wore them. Two black women moaned on the television. Makeda looked at her sneakers and wished for wings, her nose twitching at the stink of cheap booze and stale cigars.

When she heard him clear his throat, she glanced up. He was wearing a tattered bathrobe and nothing else.

"Have a little drink with me first. Night's not fit for man or beast."

She'd never get out the door before he reached her. Already he had closed to within striking distance by taking a single step. "Sure."

"Is that how you ask for it?"

"Please." She didn't have the energy to spar with him. Simply staying on her feet was a challenge, a battle he would probably be glad to see that she lost.

Grinning, he spun the top off a bottle and poured a shot into a plastic cup. "To new friends."

Makeda tried to force a smile. "New friends." She took the cup with her left hand. She'd offered herself to the clerk out of desperation, but there was a world of difference between that and this.

"I think it would be best if we waited for morning when we can see better. Don't worry. I can keep you entertained until then."

"I'm really tired, mister." The rooms on either side had been dark, but had they been empty? Would anyone hear her scream? Would anybody think he hadn't simply changed channels?

"You'll get a second wind, I promise you that. Maybe a third and fourth. Aren't you just a pretty little thing?" He lifted the bottle to his mouth.

Those had been Strick's first words to her, and she'd been too foolish to know the hurt that was coming.

"I've got to go."

He reached out and grabbed her left arm, pulled her back with him towards the bed. "We're going to have us a little party first."

"My brothers are waiting in the car. They knew I was

coming to this room." When neither fight nor flight was an option, the mind drew fancy from the sludge.

He slapped her without warning. "In that case, I don't have time to play nice." He stepped back and yanked.

Makeda's right hand went into her coat pocket, her fingers pushing past the clicking keys until she had a firm grip on the gun. She fired through the pocket, and his body tumbled onto the bed.

One shot. Nobody had responded at the apartment, and Makeda had to hope nobody would respond here either. It didn't really make any difference if they did. She was too tired to run.

If the morning, or the afternoon, if that's how long she slept, she'd use his car to jump hers, simply take it if hers wouldn't start. She'd worry about the details then.

Makeda twisted under the covers to build a cocoon, feeling the dead weight of him against her.

Sleep came easy.

Itching for Scratch

They say blondes are dumb, but then, they also say that crime doesn't pay. I meant to prove them wrong on both counts.

I'd been casing the convenience store for three weeks, long enough to see that while the cashiers might not know how to open the safe, they certainly knew how to dispense lottery scratch tickets. With my stomach growling and no more money than the pennies in my ashtray, I decided the time had come to strike.

The woman behind the counter didn't blink an eye at the gun I waved at her. "There is less than twenty dollars in the drawer, and I don't have the combination to the safe or access to the cameras that are currently recording your actions."

I motioned towards the plastic display case. "I want the scratch tickets."

She slurred her words together as she slipped into a monotone delivery. "We have one dollar tickets, two dollar tickets, and five dollar tickets. The price is marked next to the letter used to order the tickets you want."

"I want them all."

"Oh." With a shrug, she used a small key to open the side of the plastic case and handed me the contents.

Sticking the gun in my purse, I ran from the store, the cardboard streamers that promised thousands of cash prizes billowing out behind me.

I was glad to see that the parking lot was still empty. Thinking ahead, I'd parked sideways across the lines so my license plate wouldn't be captured on tape. Now I saw that someone could easily have blocked me in. I'd have to remember that for next time.

After tossing the scratch tickets into the backseat, I transferred my gun to the glove compartment so I wouldn't shoot myself reaching for a hairbrush. Then I burned rubber heading for the highway.

Unable to contain myself, I whooped, thrilled at the success of my first heist. That hadn't been so hard. Making double-sided photocopies while the boss was standing behind you was hard. This had been a breeze.

Reaching the highway, I turned north and passed the first two exits. Then I pulled off at the third and drove until I found a parking lot.

I walked around to the back seat and started organizing my haul, counting aloud as I neatly folded up the spaghetti.

There were eleven hundred and ninety-three $1 tickets.

Glancing out each of the car windows, I checked that no one had been watching while I concentrated on my addition. The parking lot was empty so it was easy to be sure.

There were nine hundred and seven $2 tickets.

Of all the different designs I'd seen so far I preferred the card with the blue diamond. It was very sharp looking with the silver trim. Most of them were just tacky.

There were two hundred and sixteen $5 tickets.

I whooped again at the extent of my haul.

All told, I had ... well ... two hundred $5 tickets was a

thousand dollars. I'd already forgotten how many $1 and $2 tickets were stacked beside me but it was a lot.

Now I just needed to convert them into cash.

Since simple plans were best I had kept my plan simple. If millions of people were willing to pay face value for lottery tickets, I shouldn't have any trouble unloading these at half price.

Returning to the front seat, I drove until I reached the nearest convenience store. Now I'd fill my pockets with an assortment of tickets and approach people on their way inside.

The first stepped around me saying, "Not interested."

The second was less polite.

The third must have ratted on me, because the manager came out and started yelling.

Undaunted, I got back on the highway. Perhaps that location had been a mistake. Instead of focusing on the competition, I should sell my stock where the tickets weren't readily available. That might make the difference.

Taking the next exit, I tried a hair salon, a bar, and a discount pharmacy.

No one was having any part of my lottery tickets. From half price I went up to face value and then for a lark I went to double price for sure-winners.

One guy asked me for a date, and another promised me life eternal. Most people just ignored me.

I tried quantity discounts, buy one get one free, and finally a free lucky scratch penny with any purchase.

As unbelievable as it seemed, I was getting nowhere.

I found one guy outside a liquor store who was willing to trade me three VCRs for the entire batch, but what the heck was I going to do with three VCRs?

Several people suggested the tickets were counterfeit, and perhaps that was the root of my problem.

All I knew for certain was that I was getting hungrier by the minute, and I only had seventeen lucky scratch pennies to my name.

Back in the car I hunted for a strip of fast food places where I was surprised to find that nobody was willing to give me a burger for ten dollars in scratch tickets, because then the drawer would be short.

What was wrong with this generation? Didn't these kids know anything? Show a little imagination.

As much as I hated the idea of using up my loot, I was going to starve to death if I didn't take a chance.

I sorted through the lucky scratch pennies until I found one born the same year as me. Then I read the instructions on a dollar ticket.

"Match your dice to any of the winning dice and win the prize shown. Reveal a snake-eye to win automatically."

I crossed my fingers and then scratched away.

No winner.

I grabbed another ticket.

No winner.

I grabbed two more.

No winner.

A buck.

I'd scratched four tickets and only won a buck. I was losing money. Even if I sold them at half face value, I would have made two bucks. And I still didn't have enough to buy something to eat.

I grabbed another handful of tickets.

No winner.

No winner.

No winner.
A buck.
No winner.
Two bucks.

I was out eleven tickets and now I was covered with sticky silver-colored dust. On the other hand, at least I had enough for the burger budget menu. Or I would once I cashed these.

Getting back on the highway, I headed for the next exit to search for another convenience store.

The heist wasn't shaping up exactly how I'd expected. My part had gone just fine, but no one else was cooperating. Didn't they realize what a great deal I was giving them?

It was just like my last job. Nobody appreciated my efforts, my ideas. They were all in such a rut. What was so great about filing alphabetically anyway?

Sighting a gas station mart, I pulled a U and turned into the parking lot and killed the engine.

After checking the losing tickets to make sure I hadn't missed something, I brought my three winners inside.

"I'd like to cash these."

The pimply kid behind the counter ran them through the machine and then froze. "The lottery is down again."

My stomach growled. "How long does it take to fix?"

"It's usually only a few minutes."

"Can you just give me the money now out of the regular drawer and then swap it later?"

The kid hesitated. "Let me check with the manager."

"Forget it." I reached for my winners.

The kid stepped back, the tickets clutched in his hand. "He's in the back room. I'm sure he'll let you have the money, but I wouldn't want to give it to you without his say-so."

Since it appeared that he might cry if I didn't agree, I said I'd wait.

As the kid scooted out from the behind the counter, I looked at all the crap on display. I couldn't sell a scratch ticket that could be worth two thousand dollars, but these ugly key chains probably moved faster than they could be replaced.

Shaking my head at the stupidity of some people, I tried to think of my next move. Maybe I needed to find a pawnshop. I'd lose money, but turning the tickets into cash was taking way too much time.

Speaking of time, where did that kid disappear to? Did he have a blonde moment or something?

I looked around the empty store.

Perhaps I should just grab some food and bolt. I could get some cookies, some chocolate bars, maybe something from the freezer I passed on the way in.

Turning to see if there were any witnesses in the parking lot, I watched a state police cruiser glide to a stop, its lights flashing.

So that's what the kid was doing in the back room. My tickets must have come up stolen on the lottery machine.

It was the story of my life. No winner.

Jumping the Fence

The waitress stopped at our table. "How is everything this evening?"

Sid smacked his lips. "The onion soup is too salty."

I watched the waitress blink as she reviewed our order. "I didn't bring you onion soup."

"No, but I've had it here before, and I doubt the recipe has improved since then."

As the waitress retreated, I shook my head. "Sid, you're in rare form this evening."

He shrugged. "What? The onion soup is too salty. She asked how everything was."

"I think she meant our meal."

"My meal was fine, because I knew enough not to order the onion soup. But what about the guy at the next table? He might be looking forward to some."

"You're a true humanitarian."

"The Pelican, on the other hand, they make an onion soup to die for. It's all in the broth."

"I'm not really a fan of onion soup."

Sid patted his chest. "You can't do better for your heart than onions."

"I exercise."

"Breaking and entering? You call that aerobic?"

"No, but dickering with you is."

"What dicker? You bring me the jewelry, and I'll give

you twenty cents on the dollar."

"Thirty."

"Twenty, and I'll pay for dinner."

"All I had was a coffee."

"We haven't left yet. Look at the dessert menu. They make a nice cheesecake here, not that they make it here."

"Sid. I can do better than twenty cents selling the pieces out of my trunk."

He smiled, touched both sides of his mouth with a napkin. "Listen, I'm on the fence with this one. A fence on a fence. That's almost funny."

"Almost."

"My grandmother, God rest her soul, was born in a country that no longer exists. You know what she told me?"

"You can't go home?"

"Wrong. Nothing. She died when my mother was three months pregnant."

I massaged a spot of sudden heartburn. "Maybe I'll have some of that onion soup after all."

"Don't bother. The salt ..." Sid shook his head. "Look, I know you're good at what you do. You break, you enter, you take, you leave. No one gets hurt. But those jewels? They're valuable, because they're unique. Unique is hard to move."

I leaned forward. "Sid, you're the best at what you do. I would not be surprised to learn you'd already found a market for the jewelry while we've been sitting here talking."

"And how would I do that?"

"Maybe you slipped the waitress a note."

"Perhaps my unused soup spoon is a radio

transmitter."

"There you go. My point is as follows. You won't have any trouble moving the jewelry, and we both know it."

"Thank you for your confidence. If you expanded your trade a little, you could be a confidence man with confidence."

"I'd rather be a thief with a fence who will give me thirty cents on the dollar."

"I never met my grandmother."

"The dead one?"

Sid nodded. "Because there are no memories to get in the way, I prefer to believe that she cares enough to send me signals from the grave."

"Like what, left turn, right turn?"

"Like stay away from this job."

A shiver went down my spine. "What do you mean?"

He sighed. "I'm on the fence. I trust you to do the job. Meanwhile, I have a bad feeling."

"Does this feeling come with any particulars?"

"My grandmother, she doesn't pretend to understand the business."

A self-appointed expert I could argue with, but a ghost who was vague? "They won't be back for two weeks. There's no one living in the house, and I can beat the alarm system. I've already been inside once."

His eyebrows lifted. "You're joking."

"This job is important to me, the score of a lifetime."

"That was risky."

"I'll do whatever I need to do in order to guarantee this job's success."

"You have to admire a man with passion."

Sid was stalling. "Thirty."

"We're arguing about pennies."

"I'll take a dollar on a dollar, if you'd rather."

Sid ignored my suggestion. "How did you get on this again?"

I sighed. "Overheard conversation at the mall. We keep discussing this, pretty soon everyone in the restaurant will know about it, too."

Sid waved away my concern. "You know who's fast to pick up on a rumor? My grandmother."

"Sid, you never met the woman."

"Death has not slowed her tongue or weakened her hearing."

At this rate, the waitress was going to return with a breakfast menu. "You're not the only fence in the city."

"If you weren't determined to work with me, then you wouldn't negotiate. What did you say, that I was one of the best in the business?"

"I said you were the best."

"I wish I had a brochure so I could add your endorsement."

Catching the eye of the waitress, I pointed at my coffee cup. "You're jerking me around, Sid."

"It's my mother's fault."

"Not your grandmother's?"

He shook his head. "My mother brought me up to be agreeable, which makes it difficult for me to disappoint you."

"What do you mean disappoint?"

"Twenty or nothing. I have a bad feeling about this job."

"Courtesy of your dead grandmother."

"She has never steered me wrong."

"So why offer twenty?"

Sid smiled. "Because I like you and the way you plan ahead. Anybody else, I wouldn't offer more than ten."

The waitress refilled my coffee, asked if we would like to order dessert. I passed, but Sid requested a piece of the cheesecake.

"You'll regret your decision when mine arrives."

"You may feel the same way when some other fence makes almost a million and a half on one deal."

Sid held out his arms. "If you feel so strongly about thirty, so be it. I wish you the best of luck."

I sat back and spun my coffee cup. With anybody but Sid handling the merchandise, I couldn't be certain nothing would go wrong at that end.

"Okay. Twenty."

Sid's cheesecake arrived along with the check, which he palmed. "I'm glad we can do business together again."

"Since I agreed to the lower cut, I'm asking you to throw in two hundred for expenses up front."

"I'll give you the money outside. And I'll pay for your coffee, but only the first cup."

"The refill is free."

"It was a joke." Sid took a bite of cheesecake. "You can loosen up now. The worst part of the job is over."

"There's still a small matter of stealing the jewelry."

"Compared to this, that will be simple. You and me, we're men of action." Sid finished his cheesecake with a flourish.

I sipped my coffee while he opened his thick billfold and laid a stack of money on the check. He tipped well, but he could afford to, paying only twenty cents on the dollar.

"All set?"

"Lead the way."

We left the restaurant and crossed the street to the parking lot where Sid opened his billfold again.

"I'll take that." A young punk appeared from the shadows, one hand outstretched and the other holding a gun. "Both of you. Your wallets and your watches."

Sid shook his head. "I don't wear a watch."

The punk stepped forward to slap Sid with the gun barrel and pulled back out of range before I could even think of a response. "Now."

I reached for my wallet while a drop of blood ran down Sid's cheek. "Sid, what's a stolen charge card worth these days?"

"Depends on the bank and security enhancements."

"Hurry up and stop yakking." He stole a glance back at the restaurant.

I pitched my wallet over the stockade fence that separated the parking lot from the field behind. "You can have that one without a fight."

He swung his gun between Sid and myself, licked his lips. "You're crazy."

"You're running out of time."

The punk broke and ran, climbed up onto a car and jumped over the fence.

Sid handed me the two hundred and put away his billfold. "I hope you didn't lose much."

"I can't say I'm looking forward to replacing my license."

Sid paused. "Okay. Thirty. I'll give you thirty for the jewelry."

"What would your grandmother say?"

"She'd say that loyalty can't be bought. It can only be

rewarded."

I grinned. "Is tomorrow night too soon?"

"That will be fine." He nodded towards the fence. "We should go before your friend decides to return."

"My friend?"

Sid placed a hand on my shoulder. "I'm the best because I know how to read people, a gift for which perhaps I should thank my dead grandmother."

"Why the offer of thirty, then?"

"Because after tomorrow I will never deal with you again, and I want our relationship to end on a happy note." Sid withdrew his hand. "You'll want to leave town, of course. If your friend was willing to throw a scare into me for two hundred, imagine what he'll do to you for three quarters of a million."

Last Call

"Are you sure this is all right?"

"Why would I lie to you?"

Dana nodded and poured herself a beer, probably the hundredth she'd poured since punching in. "The last place I tended, staff couldn't drink there even on their days off."

"Well, now you're working here. So what did you think of your first night?"

"Some of those mixed drinks threw me for a loop."

Jake wiped down the bar. "I remember when it was all just shots and drafts. Once you memorized the location of the well bottles, you could work blindfolded." He tossed the rag into the sink. "At least those layered drinks have gone out of style."

"That must have been tough."

"The pussies from the office park would come bouncing in ten minutes past quitting time and order them by the dozen. No offense."

"None taken." Dana leaned against the counter and sipped her beer. "So was tonight pretty standard?"

Jake pulled down a bottle from the top shelf and poured several inches into a water glass. "Fewer fights than usual, not that they last long. Adam's a good bouncer. He defuses the situation, unlike some other guys who have worked here."

"I was surprised to see Kevin leave so early. Doesn't the

manager usually close up?"

Jake shrugged. "We still have to check our drawers, restock, prep for tomorrow. Why should Kevin hang around twiddling his thumbs? I'll lock up, drop off the deposit, and in return treat myself to a beer on the house. Everybody's happy."

"Happy is good."

"Damn straight." Jake motioned her closer. "End of your shift, you run your reports." He turned in the key in the register to the right and hit the SALE button. The drawer popped open. "Your first report tells you how much money you should have in your drawer. Your second report is a breakdown of what you sold. Nobody looks at the second report."

The cash register started spitting out tape.

Jake sniffed. "Before you start the report, always make sure there's enough tape on the roll. I know I'm fine."

"Just at closing or even if you have a day shift?"

"Whenever you take your drawer out of the register. If Kevin asks you to fill in for half an hour, you run your reports when you're done." Jake lifted the drawer out of the register and laid it on the bar. "While that's printing, we count." He handed Dana a stack of twenties.

"Do we band them as we go?"

Jake made a face. "I don't work for the bank. The bank works for me." He handed her a deposit slip and pen. "Just jot down the totals."

Dana rifled through the twenties, glanced up to see Jake refilling his glass, continued.

Jake took the tens from the drawer. "We get paid on Tuesdays, and employees can cash their checks with us. Just treat them like money. Same with these charge card slips, except we subtract out the tips and take the money from the drawer."

Dana counted the rest of the bills and change.

"You're good with your hands," Jake said.

"I worked on an assembly line once, sorting parts."

"Why don't you total the cash and charges?"

While Dana calculated the contents of the drawer, Jake fished around for the beginning of the register tape.

He swallowed half his drink. "What do you have?"

They compared numbers.

Jake grinned. "Looks like we're over. Give me fifty-seven dollars."

Dana counted out two twenties, a ten, a five, and two ones.

Jake stuffed the money into the tip jar. "Sometimes if you're rushed, you don't spread the bills carefully enough. Someone owes you five, you see five ones, and you miss the sixth one that they meant as the tip. We catch it at the end, though."

"I suppose you could forget to ring up the drinks, too."

"What do you mean?"

"A customer orders a round of four beers. You only hit the button three times but collect the right amount because you've done it a million times. The drawer would be over then, too."

"Yeah." Jake finished his drink. "You want another?"

"No, thanks. I'll stick with this one." Dana lifted the mug. "I still have three quarters of it left."

"You got someone waiting for you at home? Afraid what will happen if you're walking a little unevenly?"

Dana shook her head. "I'm just trying to pay attention, soak everything up. Anyway, I'm not much of a drinker."

"What are you doing working in a bar?"

She smiled. "I've got nothing against people who drink. It just makes me lightheaded. Think of all the money I'm saving."

"Sure." Jake wiped his mouth. "So after you take care of your drawers, it's time to restock. We replace the bottles we emptied and fill the beer coolers."

"And the liquor is stored downstairs, right?"

"Glad you've been paying attention." Jake pulled an empty box from beneath the bar. "We bring the bottles down with us."

Dana gathered the empty bottles that stood along the floor, conscious of Jake watching the front of her shirt as she worked. "What do we do about the empty beer bottles?"

"They stay out back where we put them."

She stood. "That's it."

"Let's go."

Jake took the box and led Dana through the kitchen to a padlocked door. "You'll get your own key." He unlocked the door and flicked on the switch before leading her downstairs. "Every so often we have trouble with rats or mice. Just don't get your panties in an uproar."

"I'll try to remember that."

"Hard liquor is stored on these shelves over here. You'll notice the bottles are in rows by type and brand with a row of empty bottles between them. The first thing Kevin does when he comes in is count all the bottles."

Jake placed the box on the floor and pulled out a bottle. The empty went on a shelf and a full one replaced it in the box.

"What if a bottle gets thrown out by accident?"

"Kevin has a heart attack. Honestly, if you break a bottle, send a customer to the liquor store for a replacement and pour the booze down the drain. It's worth the expense to keep Kevin off your back."

"Is he hard to work for?"

"He's an idiot." Jake lifted the box, now filled with full bottles. "Do you think you can carry this upstairs?"

Dana took the box from him. "I'm stronger than I look."

"I'll get a couple cases of beer. They're over on those pallets."

Jake motioned Dana up the stairs before him. "After you."

Back behind the bar, Jake told her to start restocking while he went downstairs for more beer.

Dana placed the hard liquor in the cabinets under the bar, stacked beers in the coolers. She straightened the bottles on the shelves, facing the labels.

Jake returned with two more cases of beer, and she put them away, too.

He picked up his drink. "Some people bring a change of clothes. You know, once the last customer leaves, you can slip into something a little more comfortable."

"The uniform is just fine."

Jake snorted. "Sometimes it gets wet, smelly. Wait until your first customer pukes on you. You'll wish you'd thrown a nice little halter top into your bag."

"So now what do we do?"

"You put the chairs on the tables, and I'll put the deposit together. That's the slip, the money, and any payroll checks. Bottom copy of the deposit slip goes in the empty register drawer along with the two reports and the charge card slips."

Dana started putting up chairs. "Do we sweep or anything?"

"There's a young hottie comes in to do that kind of stuff in the morning. I saw her once on my way out."

"Couldn't get the drawer to balance?"

Jake grinned. "Couldn't decide which was better, ten-year old Scotch or fifty-year old whiskey."

"I hope Kevin didn't catch you."

"He couldn't catch venereal disease. Kevin gets shot down trying to masturbate." Jake laughed. "I've seen him approach women I've been pouring drinks into all night. He'd have trouble picking up a ten dollar whore."

"Maybe he's not trying to hit on them. Maybe he's just checking to see if the customers are satisfied."

"Then how come he never talks to the guys?"

"Maybe because you don't comp the guys drinks." Dana winked at him.

"No flies on you." Jake toasted her with his glass.

"That's it for the chairs."

"Last call. You ready for another drink?"

"No thanks."

"Why don't you come back here, and we'll figure out what we're going to do about the tips."

Dana rejoined him behind the bar.

Jake emptied the tip jar. "You probably noticed during the night that whenever I had a free second, I was going through the tip jar and exchanging silver and small bills for tens and twenties. That way the drawer always has enough to make change and I'm not going home with a four-inch wallet and a pocket hanging down to my knees."

"Yes, I did see that."

"Call you Eagle Eye." Jake sorted the bills. "Now, this

was a training shift for you, which means no tips."

"Okay."

"I don't feel so good about it myself. I mean, were you working here tonight, or were you working?"

"I was working."

"Damn straight. Here's a hundred dollars."

"Thanks." Dana folded the money into her pocket.

"Don't tell Kevin I gave it to you."

"It's our little secret."

"You sure you don't want another drink? You did real good tonight."

"I'd doze off on the way home."

"You can't go home just yet."

"I thought we were done."

Jake reached up and started killing the lights until the only illumination came from neon signs. "Done working maybe."

"No, it's late. I've got to be going."

"Why rush home to an empty bed? Kevin's going to ask how you did tonight. I'd rather not disappoint him."

"Sorry. Not interested."

"I think you will be. That hundred in your pocket, it belongs in the deposit bag. The bank's gonna want to know why the amount doesn't match what you wrote on the slip."

"You're making a mistake."

"Didn't I see you shortchange two customers? The bar might have to press charges to protect our good name." Jake stepped closer to Dana, placed his hand on her arm.

He spun her around, pushing her head down onto the bar, pressing himself against her. "The way I see this, you've got two choices. You get to pick which one I use."

Dana reached back, grabbed his balls, and squeezed.

As Jake screamed, Dana turned and punched him in the throat.

"Let's end this now before I have to hurt you."

Jake gurgled, staggered, and dropped to the floor.

"You misjudge Kevin. He looks at those second reports and compares them to liquor levels. He talks to customers you ply with free drinks and pressure for sex. He notices the shortages." Dana stepped over Jake and flipped on the lights again. "He'll be here in a few minutes to call the police. You can apologize then."

Jake dragged himself to a sitting position. "You a cop?"

"Private investigator."

"Oh, shit."

"I'm also an experienced witness. Even if your lawyer blocks the video gathered by the cameras I installed, you probably want to confess and plead out, because I'll bury you on the stand."

At the sound of the front door opening, Dana smiled. "Here's Kevin now."

Officer Down

As soon as he saw the flashing lights in his rearview mirror, Dent glanced down at the speedometer to confirm he was safely under the speed limit. Only then did he pull to the side of the road.

The police cruiser stopped behind him.

While Dent knew that some private investigators had trouble with the local law, he had managed to avoid that complication. He didn't interfere with their business, and they left him alone. Of course, today might prove the exception that changed the rule.

Dent brought down his window. "Afternoon, Officer." The cop was young, probably just out of the academy.

"Dent."

"Have we met?"

The officer shook his head. "Mind if I join you?"

"Be my guest." Dent unlocked the passenger door wondering whether the cop wanted access in order to plant evidence of some sort. If so, why? He was working three cases, but none of them should have given the police cause for concern.

The officer sat and closed the door behind him before holding out his hand. "The name's Lester."

Dent shook. "What can I do for you, Officer Lester?"

"Are you wearing a wire?"

"Nope."

"I'll trust you. I have to trust you."

Dent shared the sentiment since the PI was alone with an armed man on a desolate stretch of road, a man who could shoot first and falsify reports later. "You want to tell me what this is about?"

"Not really, but I don't have any choice. The Chief sent me to hunt you down. He knew it wouldn't be wise for him to contact you directly."

"I'm on my way to interview a witness. Every minute I'm delayed, the fuzzier the memory becomes."

Officer Lester pursed his lips. "Odd things have been happening, and the Chief is concerned that rogue cops might be involved."

"What kinds of things?"

"Bag men and drug dealers killed, their money taken. The Chief says there's no evidence of a turf war. The targets are too random, and the streets have been quiet."

"So why does he suspect his own people?"

"Who better than a cop knows what's what?"

It made sense. Dent was familiar with the temptations a cop faced. "And how are you involved?"

"I'm the new guy. The Chief took me aside yesterday for the usual welcome aboard speech and laid this on me." Lester sighed. "I'm just trying to fit in and learn the ropes. You know?"

Dent nodded. "If anyone finds out what you're doing, they'll make your life miserable. If they don't just kill you outright."

"The thought has crossed my mind."

"So what does the Chief want with me?"

"He wants someone outside the department to investigate. You're an investigator."

Dent stared out the windshield. "He wants me to find the dirty cops?"

"The Chief doesn't know who he can trust."

"And he thinks he can trust me?"

"I guess." Lester appeared confused. "Is there any reason he shouldn't?"

Dent smiled. "I used to wear the uniform a long time ago. When my wife developed cancer, I needed money, and certain people were willing to give it to me if I looked the other way when they asked."

"You were crooked?"

"The quick answer is, yes. The truth is, I only wanted to keep the love of my life alive. That's why it didn't go to trial. The Chief gave me the option of resigning, and I did. And then she died anyway,"

"I'm sorry."

"You can see why I'm a little surprised by this."

"Maybe the Chief figures your experience is an advantage."

"Send a dirty cop to find a dirty cop."

"Something like that."

Dent rubbed his ear. "I couldn't keep an investigation like this quiet. The people I'd have to talk to, they aren't Freedom of Information clerks."

"The Chief understands the situation. He told me that if you didn't solve this within twenty-four hours, you never would."

"I suppose he has decided I can simply ignore my other clients, paying clients, clients who have their own sense of urgency."

Officer Lester winced but continued. "He's asking for those twenty-four hours. Ferret out the corruption before they hear you coming and throw up walls, destroy evidence, take care of loose ends."

"What can you give me for background?"

"The files are in my cruiser. The Chief wasn't sure you'd take the job."

"No matter what the Chief told you, I don't have a choice. Any more than you did."

"So I can tell him you'll conduct the investigation?"

"You can tell him that we're even, and I expect to be paid as soon as I hand him my report. That will be five thousand dollars, in case he needs to transfer funds between line items."

Officer Lester whistled. "Going private pays well."

"The circumstances are highly unusual."

"What if it's too much?"

Dent grinned. "Then you can tell the Chief to arrest me for highway robbery. I won't take the job for a penny less."

Officer Lester opened his mouth but finally only shrugged and opened his door. "Let's go get the files."

After taking possession of the thick manila envelope and driving away from the newest addition to the force, Dent called his appointment to reschedule the interview for the day after tomorrow.

While he didn't say so to the witness, he thought, *that is, if I haven't been shot for resisting arrest.*

Cops, whether good or bad, for good or bad, hung together. If Dent managed to solve this case without being killed, he would make life-long enemies. Even the cleanest cops would never forgive him.

Sure, the Chief would be in his corner. That might help a little until the top cop decided to run for public office or teach history to high school students.

Five thousand was high for a day's work but low for a lifetime of harassment. Dent might just have to investigate transferring his license to another state and starting all over again. He knew what cops could be like.

Dent drove to the Blue Buzzard and ordered a late lunch before opening the manila envelope.

There were about fifteen sheets of paper, laser printed, each with a photograph clipped to the corner.

Dent drank his coffee while he read.

He was holding brief biographies of area hoodlums. Included were places of frequency, schedules, and guards. Personal firearms were noted, as was history of wearing protection.

Seven of the sheets had an X in the upper right-hand corner. Dent recognized some of the names. These were the targets who had already been hit.

The waitress arrived with his sandwich. "Can I bring you anything else?"

"Thanks. I'll send up a flare when I can use a refill on the coffee."

Dent slowly chewed his BLT. He had expected the envelope to contain police reports on the dead men. While a list of possible future targets might allow him to catch the killer in the act, Dent wondered who compiled the information.

Why bother gathering details on the dead men unless the Chief was hoping to find a connection? Nothing had jumped out at Dent yet, but he would have liked to know more.

Who was the first cop on the scene? Who ran each of the investigations? Who were friends with whom, the cliques within the clique?

Were all the hoodlums killed with the same weapon? When were they killed? Where?

The information was great, but Dent needed more.

While he couldn't call the Chief, perhaps he could reach Lester to act the part of the mule and deliver copies of the police reports. Dent simply didn't have time to sift through newspaper accounts of the killings, searching for details that probably never appeared in print.

Dent wiped his mouth, pushed the empty plate away. He had learned long ago not even to leave the crumbs behind when he wasn't sure how soon he'd eat again.

As soon as he started asking questions on the street, the clock would start ticking. He'd be lucky if he had twenty-four hours. He might not have half that.

With cops involved, the trail could go cold and evaporate in less time than it took for a bullet to find its mark.

The waitress returned with a coffee pot, posed at the edge of Dent's table. "Did you hear?"

"Hear what?"

"Someone killed a cop over on Old County Road."

Old County was where he left Lester. "That's terrible. Did they catch the people responsible?"

The waitress took Dent's coffee cup and refilled it. "Not according to the news. It didn't even sound as though there were any suspects. Really, when the cops aren't safe, what chance do the rest of us have?"

"Things get worse every day. I'll take the check when it's ready."

"I'll just go add it up."

Dent scooted his papers into the manila envelope.

Did the rogue cops catch up with Lester? Did they

know Dent had been hired and was holding this information? If they were willing to kill one of their own, then they wouldn't hesitate to waste a nosy private detective.

Back in his car, Dent called the police business line and asked to speak to the Chief.

"I'm sorry, but he's not in this afternoon."

"Can you beep him for me?"

"He's out of town on a fishing trip. Would you like to talk with Captain Prescott?"

"No, thanks. How soon do you expect the Chief back?"

"Not for a couple of days."

Dent disconnected. With one of his cops killed, the Chief was probably already halfway home.

Unless ... how far would the rogue cops go to protect themselves? They'd already killed seven hoods and Officer Lester. Would they risk taking out the Chief?

Dent flipped through his address book until he found Troy's number.

"This is Dent."

"Hey, did you hear about that cop getting shot?"

Dent sniffed. "A waitress brought me the news with my coffee. Listen, you play cards with the Chief. Do you know where he likes to fish?"

"It depends."

"On what?" Troy was the Public Works Director, and Dent once brought his teenage daughter back from Vegas.

"Creature comforts."

"Again? In English?"

"If he's going alone, he stays at the Crown Hotel and fishes at the nearby lake. If there's a party of us, we stay at his cabin on Long Pond. Otherwise, he takes his camper out to a place on the river."

"I didn't know they were restocking the Gooseneck."

"They aren't."

The Chief was a widower, but his late wife had been widely popular and the reason for his public support before she was killed in a car accident. Maybe in another five or six years, he'd be allowed to date again. "Does otherwise have a name?"

"Is it important?"

"I think the Chief might be in danger."

"Is this related to the cop that was shot?"

"I'm afraid so."

Troy sighed. "Marilyn Housner. The library director. And you didn't hear it from me."

Dent called the library and learned the director was on vacation. Gooseneck River it was.

He laid down the telephone and started his car.

Around the turn of the century, the previous century, Gooseneck River had been home to revival meetings. While the few permanent buildings had long been razed, the clearing was never reclaimed by the wild. Kids, and apparently at least one chief of police, found a new use for the property.

Dent turned on the radio and hit area stations to see if there was an update on the shooting. He heard three different versions of tomorrow's weather and a nearly insufferable amount of inane banter.

While stopped at the intersection of Arlington and Vine, Dent found himself facing a police cruiser.

The officer hit the lights and siren.

Dent gunned the engine and jumped the curb to bang a right onto Arlington.

He took the next right and then the first left.

Sparing a second to look in the mirror he saw the cruiser fishtail around the last corner.

Dent accelerated, let up on the gas, and then hooked a left without braking.

He slid into an open parking spot and killed the engine as he dropped to the seat.

The siren came closer, passed, disappeared into the distance.

Dent slowly sat and peered through the windshield. Sensing the coast was clear, he made a U-turn and took the long way to Gooseneck.

Officer Maloney was a bad cop and a so-so driver. Dent wasn't surprised that Maloney was the first to be added to the list of possible rogue cops. Even back when Dent carried a badge, Maloney gave off a smell that no amount of cologne could cover.

And if Dent remembered correctly, Maloney tried.

Cindy had never cared much for the other cops. Most of the civilian wives and husbands didn't. Even the mere mention of Maloney, however, caused Cindy to wrinkle her nose. "Don't ever cross that one."

Cindy would not have been happy with this case.

Dent wasn't too fond of it himself.

He was watching his mirror more than he was paying attention to the road ahead, waiting to see flashing lights, the beginning of the end. Maloney could have easily spun some story to the dispatcher, accused Dent of any crime from attempted robbery to hit and run. Armed and dangerous. Fired on a police officer. Use extreme caution.

Getting shot by an honest cop didn't make you any less dead.

Dent doubled the speed limit and then passed it.

He should have asked Lester for the Chief's personal phone number, but then, Lester should have given it to him without prompting.

Did the Chief suspect the rogue cops were collecting information by monitoring telephone calls? Was that even still possible? Dent wished he spent more time keeping up on the evolving technologies, but if he did, he wouldn't have a moment for anything else.

Finally reaching Old Post Road, Dent floored the accelerator. Now he spent more time scanning the road ahead, searching for a possible ambush.

The only thing working to his advantage was that they couldn't simply shoot the Chief. Nobody would buy a hunting accident this far out of season in an area that rarely saw game. The rogue cops would have to try to be clever, and clever took time.

Dent came around a corner to find a large branch blocking half the road. He tapped his brakes, started to skid, turned into it and regained control. After no one appeared to take advantage of the surprise, Dent decided the branch wasn't a trap, simply another job for Public Works.

Why hadn't Troy given Dent the Chief's number? They played cards and fished together. The Chief wouldn't withhold the number from such a close friend, and Troy shouldn't have kept it a secret when the Chief's life was in danger.

Did Dent slow enough to call Troy back or continue driving at break-neck speed? Could he accomplish more by calling the Chief or arriving on the scene? What if Troy still refused to share the information?

Dent kept the pedal to the floor.

If Troy was involved, the bad guys knew Dent was concerned about the Chief's safety. They knew where Dent was headed.

The Chief was probably in that hotel ordering room service, the librarian sitting down by the indoor pool. Dent was rushing to a secluded area where the rogue cops wouldn't be disturbed during their interrogation of him. Or the burial afterwards.

Dent wavered, lifting his foot from the accelerator.

Why would Troy lie? Dent had saved his daughter. What could the Director of Public Works offer to the rogue cops in exchange for diluting everybody's share?

Dent pressed his foot down again.

Preparing for whatever lay ahead, Dent tried to recall the layout of the revival grounds. He seemed to remember two roads winding their way in through the woods, the clearing nestled in a crook of the river and surrounded on three sides by water, nothing worth calling high ground.

Of course, he hadn't been there in years. Decades. Given the current spate of development, he probably shouldn't be surprised to find a four-lane highway leading to a three-story mall.

Dent went flying past the first entrance.

Swearing, he slowed and pulled over to the shoulder in order to make a three-point turn. As soon as he pulled onto the entry road, he stopped the car, lowered his window, and turned off the engine.

Birds. Squirrels. Something that sounded like it belonged in a South American jungle.

He didn't hear gunfire, and he didn't hear sirens.

Dent started his car and inched down the road.

This was prime ambush territory, the road narrow and the woods thick. Dent's gaze darted from spot to spot, searching for a tale-tell sign of trouble. He drove with his left hand and held his gun in his right.

Dent paid so much attention to the journey that he was shocked when he reached his destination. There on the far side of the clearing was the Chief's camper. No other vehicles were visible.

Dent stopped his car and slowly stepped out onto the leafy ground. He turned a slow circle and jumped when a bird took off with a squawk.

The door to the camper opened, and Housner came into view, dressed in bra and panties. Dent lowered his gun.

"Stop right there."

Dent recognized the voice that came from behind him as the Chief's. "It's me, Dent."

"I know who it is." Housner closed the camper door, mission accomplished.

"Can I turn around?"

"First, lose the gun."

Dent laid his weapon on the ground and then faced the Chief. "You're alive."

"You're under arrest."

"What?"

"They lifted your prints off Lester's car. I know you've had your troubles, but I never thought you'd kill a cop."

Dent remembered leaning against the cruiser while waiting for Officer Lester to retrieve the manila envelope. "I didn't kill anyone. Officer Lester was sitting in his car sipping a coffee when I left him."

"According to his radio calls, he chased you for three

miles and finally forced you off the road before you'd stop."

Dent licked his lips. "It wasn't like that at all. Officer Lester flashed his lights, I pulled over, and he joined me in my car to tell me about your need for a private investigator."

"What need?"

"You didn't send Lester to me?"

The Chief shook his head. "Keep talking."

"Lester said you suspected some officers had gone rogue, killing hoods for the cash on hand. He hired me in your name."

"This is all news to me."

Dent rubbed his ear. "If you didn't hire me, who did? Maybe no one did. Maybe I was being set up."

"Do you have any proof to back up what you're saying?"

"I have the files Officer Lester gave me. They should have his prints on them, and he must have touched inside surfaces of my car, as well as the passenger door handle." Dent paused. "I also have a verbal agreement that you'll pay me five thousand to solve the case."

The Chief cracked a smile. "Lester obviously never saw my budget. Maybe I could spare you five hundred, but you'd also have to paint the hallways."

Dent waited for the Chief to holster his gun before retrieving his own. "Is it possible you have some rogue cops operating in the department?"

"That would explain certain things." The Chief exhaled. "No one has suggested the possibility, though. You think they shot Lester?"

"It's all that makes sense. He was the pawn who drew

me onto the playing field. Then he was sacrificed."

"Why frame you?"

"Good question. I'm an ex-cop. I know what's what. I'm private, which means I'll draw attention away from possible police involvement."

"You're the perfect patsy."

"The only question is, why now? It doesn't sound as though the department was breathing down their neck. Once they complete their frame of me, they shut down their own operation."

"What are you going to do?"

"I nail the bad cops before they nail me in a coffin. I don't think I have time to wait for you to begin an internal investigation."

"First, I'd have to know who I could trust."

Dent nodded. "That's what I figured. Hey, why were you waiting out here with a gun, your friend inside with her underwear?"

"Troy called me and said you were coming. When he heard about the Lester shooting, Troy called Prescott, who suggested you were the prime suspect."

"He did, did he? That's interesting."

The Chief shook his head and held up a hand. "Don't jump to any conclusions. Lester's last radio calls involved pulling you over. Your prints were on his car. I'd make the same assumption."

Dent opened his door. "So would the person who set me up."

Leaving the Chief walking towards his camper, Dent reassessed the situation as he drove away from the clearing.

Everything Lester said was in doubt. Well, not

everything. The hoods were killed, their money taken, and cops were likely suspects. Perhaps he only lied when he mentioned the Chief and when he omitted who really sent him.

The rogue cops convinced the new kid on the block to mislead Dent. Maybe they told Lester it was a practical joke, or maybe they told him it was part of a sting operation. In any case, Lester played his role, and Dent took the bait.

Dent turned onto Old Post Road and headed towards town.

Why did they kill Lester? For one thing, it was a crime to pin on Dent. For another, it wasn't particularly easy to turn a rookie who still believed in the sanctity of the system. Lester might have signed on and then changed his mind.

Killing one of their own was an extreme measure, but this time, it made sense.

They waited until the Chief was gone fishing before sending Lester after Dent with the fake hiring act. Dent kills Lester. A cop kills Dent. The contents of the manila folder finger Dent as the culprit in the recent murders. End of story.

So why was Dent free? If he wasn't shot trying to escape, the whole plan fell apart. The longer Dent lived, the looser the frame fit. Did they ever imagine in their worst-case scenarios that he might actually talk to the Chief?

Dent pulled to the side of the road when he realized he wasn't paying enough attention to his driving. If there was one thing he didn't need right now, it was a minor accident stranding him out here.

They probably didn't know he'd talked to the Chief. Would that make a difference to their plan either way?

If they thought the Chief knew, they'd probably take the manila folder after they killed Dent to take the wind from the sails of any internal investigation.

If they thought the Chief didn't know, they'd leave the manila folder so Dent could be blamed for the other killings.

In either case, Dent had to be silenced.

Unfortunately, Dent couldn't imagine any sequence of events where it wasn't in the best interest of the rogue cops to kill him and, except for Maloney, he didn't even know who they were.

Could he play Maloney? Should he shake Captain Prescott and see what fell out? Just how many cops were part of the conspiracy?

Dent slapped the steering wheel. He should have told the Chief whether or not to clear his name. Which would be better?

On the one hand, he wouldn't need to worry about being gunned down by an honest cop. On the other hand, the bad cops would know the game was up.

It would help to know what the Chief decided to do.

Dent turned his car around and headed to Gooseneck. He should have asked the Chief for his phone number when they were face to face, just like he should have asked Lester enough questions to reveal the charade.

And possibly, if he had done everything different from the day he was born, Cindy would still be alive.

Dent missed the entrance again, but this time he laughed at his mistake, backing up and then taking the road at normal speed. Since the Chief hadn't really hired him, Dent didn't need to worry about being ambushed here.

Just what had gone wrong for the rogues earlier? One cop would have been enough for Lester, and another should have stopped Dent farther down the road. Why had he been allowed to leave the scene? The danger of him talking outweighed any issues of a believable stop.

They could have killed Lester and Dent at the same time and concocted some story to fit the facts. Something too farfetched might raise a few eyebrows, but in the end, it would still suffice.

Their whole plan hinged on killing him. If he lived, they were sunk. If he lived long enough to talk, they were sunk.

Sure, they might have been scrambled to respond to an armed robbery, but if that was true, he would have heard something.

At the time they should have been pumping him full of lead, he had been in the Blue Buzzard eating lunch. Someone messed up badly, and that was a sign of an organization in trouble.

Dent entered the clearing, saw the camper on the far side, a body lying on the ground in front of it.

He hit the brakes, rolled out of his car with a gun in his hand. He came up quickly and spun a three-sixty.

There was no sign of any movement in the woods or the camper.

Dent slowly made his way toward the body, his eyes never resting for long, his senses heightened as he probed for threats.

Nobody had passed him. That meant that either the killer was still here or had taken the second road. So there might have been a trap after all, the hunter gambling on which road Dent would take and guessing wrong.

As Dent came closer to the body, he started to give more of his attention to the camper. There was the door and a small curtained window. The curtain wouldn't stop a bullet any more than the glass would.

Dent reached the body, kneeled next to it without taking his eye off the camper. His hand fumbled until he found the neck, searched for a pulse but it was long gone.

Risking a glance down, Dent saw that the Chief had been shot once. Sometimes once was all it took.

He stood and walked toward the camper. "Marilyn?"

She could be frightened. She could be dead. She could be the one who pulled the trigger.

Dent rapped on the door. Then he stood to the side and yanked it open.

When nothing happened, he entered.

The camper was empty.

Dent spent a few minutes searching to see whether Marilyn's things were still there. They were. Then he got ready to leave.

First he moved behind the door and took a deep breath.

Then he pushed it open and dove down and left, coming up to a crouch with gun in hand.

He was still alone in the clearing.

Dent stood, lowering his gun but keeping it ready. He'd rather look like a fool than a corpse any day.

After pausing to pay his respects to the Chief, Dent returned to his car.

A private investigator could easily turn paranoid, convince himself that Marilyn was guilty, as was Troy, as was Captain Prescott. Everybody was a threat.

That was a dangerous place where investigations could be derailed and innocent people hurt.

On the other hand, someone had killed Officer Lester. Someone had killed the Chief. The world might not be peopled by devils, but it wasn't peopled by angels either.

Lester's telephone rang. The number was blocked.

"Hello?"

"This is Maloney. We need to talk."

"I'm listening."

"Not on the telephone. The Bracken Motel. Room nineteen."

"People will know I'm coming."

"That's fine."

Dent disconnected and tossed his telephone onto the passenger seat. Who would he tell?

After calculating the shortest route, Dent decided on one a little more circuitous. Maloney could have been calling from anywhere. He could be around the next corner, him and the rest of his gang, guns raised and safeties off.

If there was a single lesson Dent had learned on the streets, it was that the time to relax never came. Drop your guard, and take a bullet.

Lie on a hammock soaking up the bright summer afternoon without a care in the world. Learn your wife has cancer. Oops, I guess you shouldn't have closed your eyes.

Life kicked you when you were down. It pushed you down, it kicked you, and then it drew a gun.

Shaking the dark thoughts from his head, Dent concentrated on his driving. Lester had been a stranger, but Dent had known the Chief for years. While they weren't exactly friends, in some ways they were more.

Cindy had been fond of saying, "A bird in the hand gathers no moss." Dent never knew what she meant, and when he asked, she only laughed.

Right now he thought the phrase meant: "Focus on what you have." What he had was Maloney.

Dent stopped at a light, watched the three other approaches.

Why Maloney wanted to meet was a mystery. Dent needed to turn the probable trap into an opportunity. Cindy's assessment of the man might well prove the ticket.

Dent would tell Maloney that the reason Dent was still walking around was that the rogues had decided to cut him in. So as to not lessen their shares, they were planning to cut Maloney out, permanently.

The light changed and Dent continued.

If he knew Maloney, the cop would run hot until the blood of the double-crossers ran cold. Then it would simply be a matter of picking up the pieces to complete the puzzle.

The only question was whether Maloney would give Dent a chance to talk. If the cop shot Dent through the motel room door it would put a serious crimp in the plan.

There was also the slight chance that Maloney had been the one fingered to kill Dent. In that case, Maloney would know why he hadn't completed the contract and could now try, try again.

Dent was smarter than Maloney and probably better with a gun. He had to hope his edge would cancel Maloney's home turf advantage.

The tough part would be convincing Maloney that Dent was now a player when he didn't know square one.

Just ahead was the Bracken Motel, the sign in pink and white neon, half the letters out.

Dent passed the entrance to the parking lot, looking for anything suspicious. Nothing jumped out at him.

He returned to the Bracken and parked next to the office, went inside and asked for the location of room nineteen.

It was an end unit, ground floor, and Dent walked towards the room with his hand in his pocket. There was no point in advertising he had a gun. Maybe Maloney wouldn't be so fast to shoot before Dent had a chance to spin his tale.

He slowed as he came with twenty feet. The one big window had curtains drawn.

Dent quickened his pace to throw off the aim of anyone who had been watching.

Standing to the side of the door, he knocked.

The door swung open, and Dent smelled the whiskey before he saw Maloney.

The cop waved Dent into the room. "Whatever you expected, you're wrong. My gun's on the dresser." Maloney sat on the bed, retrieved a half-empty whiskey bottle from the floor.

Dent turned the desk chair to face the bed, started right in. "Your friends have made me an offer."

"My friends."

"They said that someone outside the force could be useful to them. They've asked me to join."

Maloney tipped the bottle back and chugged. After wiping his mouth, he winced and turned towards Dent. "Why do you think I asked you here?"

"You mean, you expected the double-cross?"

He laughed. "You've got nerve, I'll give you that. Listen, I have no friends. Literally."

"It's just business."

"That's not what I meant." Maloney took a deep breath. "The whole enchilada, it's a one-man show, Maloney Productions. I've been killing creeps for their cash, the last desperate ploy of a short-timer, but I retire in eighty-seven days. I couldn't stop before the case was closed, and then I remembered you."

"You're the one who sent me Officer Lester."

Maloney shook his head. "Why are they putting college kids in uniform? Lester didn't belong on the street. He wouldn't have survived a year."

"So you helped him out by shortening it."

Maloney's shoulders slumped. "I needed someone to set you up. You were perfect. Everybody knew why you left the force. And yes, I killed him."

"How did you convince him to go along with your plan?" Dent watched Maloney to make sure he didn't pull a second gun out of hiding.

"I told him you were the prime suspect in the shootings, and we were going to screw with your head, see if we could force you to make a mistake." He took another hit from the bottle.

"The radio calls?"

"The kid was so excited to be part of his first big case that he didn't ask questions. He was book smart but not too bright. Even when I had my gun on him, he was wagging his tail until the second I pulled the trigger." Maloney paused. "And then I lost you."

"I took the cut-through to the Blue Buzzard."

He nodded. "I figured out later that must have been it,

but by the time I reached the restaurant, you were gone. I raced all over town looking for you."

"You saw me once."

"And then I lost you a second time. I should have retired years ago, supplemented my pension with some security job instead of holding out until the last minute."

"You killed the Chief."

A sob escaped Maloney. "I was in a panic when I saw your car on Old Post. I followed you up to the Chief's camper, shot him after you left, told his lady librarian that you killed him just before I arrived. I thought I had regained the situation, but I was wrong. She's in room twenty-four, upstairs. I told her she was in protective custody."

"And then you called me."

"You're in the book." He nodded towards the listings that lay open on the desk. "I never meant to shoot the Chief. Lester, I could live with. Not the Chief."

"The frame you built was falling apart."

"Maybe, if I could just kill you quick before you talked to anyone else ... but not after shooting the Chief. I couldn't live with a mistake like that." Maloney was holding the whiskey bottle in both hands, staring at the amber liquid as if searching for absolution.

Dent stood. "It's over now. I'll bring you in."

"No. I couldn't live with that either." Maloney looked up with empty eyes. "You're an ex-cop. You understand."

"I do."

"What can I say? Things spun out of control, went from bad to worse in a heartbeat. I was so close to making it all work." Maloney cleared his throat. "She's in twenty-four. Tell her I'm sorry. He was a good man."

Dent nodded, glanced at Maloney's gun sitting on the dresser, and closed the motel room door behind him.

Dent was halfway up the outside staircase when he heard the single muffled shot.

One-Eyed Jacks

"Deal already."

"Shaddup."

"Guys, let's just cool it."

"Not even Mike's deal."

Mike continued to shuffle with certain hands. "It's my turn. Dealer's choice."

Ned groaned. "This isn't going to be another one of your screwy games, is it? Drink up everybody. We're going to need fortification."

Mike placed a card face down in front of Ned. "It's called Jack-off."

"You're joking."

Mike placed cards in front of Omar, Paul, and himself. "Each player gets one card face down. Then I deal the rest face up."

"What's the object?"

"If you receive a black card, you chug a shot of Jack." Mike reached down and slammed a full bottle onto the table.

"What if you get a red card?"

"You do a double."

"Sounds like a good game to me."

"What's the object?"

"You already asked him that."

"Did he answer?"

"I think so."

Mike dealt one card face up to each player, naming the card as he flipped it over. "Ned has the two of diamonds. Omar has the three of clubs. Paul has the queen of diamonds. Dealer has seven of spades."

After uncapping the bottle, Mike passed it to his left. "Drink up and then toss in a white chip."

The bottle went around the table until four chips sat in the middle.

"So how does someone win, or do we just stop when we run out of booze?"

Ned grinned. "We stop when Rachel calls and asks me when I'm going to be home."

"Don't keep her up too late." Omar tried to focus on his watch. "I need her to finish typing that report first thing."

Mike lowered the deck to his lap and slipped it into his left pocket, taking the one he'd fixed from his right. "The game is up when the fourth jack is exposed. Every time a jack comes into play, the person who receives it has to do something."

"I was afraid of this."

"If you pull a jack, you have to spill a secret, something you've never told anyone, especially the rest of us."

"This sounds like a girl game."

"As a matter of fact, I learned it from my sister."

"Rachel never mentioned it to me."

"We played it a long time ago, when we were just kids. You didn't even know her yet."

"Let's go already."

Mike dealt. "Ned has the six of clubs. Omar has the queen of clubs. Paul has the ace of hearts. Dealer has the jack of clubs."

"You got a jack."

Mike passed the bottle. "First everybody drink. Then I'll tell my secret."

The three others chugged quickly and added their white chip to the pile. Mike moved more slowly and then wiped his mouth with the back of his hand before speaking.

"Jack of clubs. That's violence." He sighed. "This happened about two years ago. I was parked along Wisconsin. It was late, getting dark. The stores were closing. All of a sudden, in the rearview mirror, I saw someone push this old lady down and grab her purse. She must have said something, because he kicked her. Then he started running toward me. I didn't even think. I leaned over the passenger seat, unlocked the door, and pushed it open just as he reached my car. Bam. He hit the door and went down."

Mike tapped the jack of clubs. "I jumped out and proceeded to kick the crap out of him. I knew that even if he hadn't hurt her, he'd altered the woman's life forever. I knew that even if he was arrested, found guilty, and sentenced, that his punishment would never affect him as much as his crime had affected her. So I became his punishment."

The other players were silent until Ned finally swore.

Omar added, "So what happened?"

"I drove the old lady home. The next day, there was a news story about the assault with no known witnesses. The victim was in intensive care. Then I never really heard anything else."

"Why didn't you tell us?"

"I didn't want to involve you all. Make you accessories

to what I'd done. It does feel good to admit the truth, though. That night was like a dream, a dream I felt I couldn't share because it was such a nightmare."

Ned clapped his shoulder. "Hey, you helped the lady."

Omar nodded. "That's right. She could have been hurt. Or he might have decided there wasn't enough money in the purse and gone back for her. Sick world."

"So that's my secret. For what it's worth." Mike picked up the deck and started to deal. "Time to play. Ned has the seven of spades. Omar has the ten of clubs. Paul has the ace of clubs. Dealer has the ten of diamonds. Drink up."

Two more sets of cards were dealt before the next jack appeared. Omar pulled the diamond. "What was that again?"

"Money. Once we all chug and ante, tell us some crime you committed for money."

"Omar?"

"Everybody has secrets. That's why we play the game."

They drank, tossed in their chip, and then Omar stared across the table at Mike. "Okay. It involves Mike. Seven months ago, my car was in the garage, and my brother called in a panic. I couldn't get a cab to take me out of state, the rental places were closed, and I finally got ahold of Mike. He swung by, and I dropped him off."

Omar took a deep breath. "My brother was really in trouble. He needed money, and he needed it fast. He sat there crying in Mike's car. I opened the glove compartment, looking for tissues or something, and I found an envelope filled with cash. I took it because I needed it. I never said anything because I was embarrassed, and I couldn't pay it back without letting you know. I'm sorry. I can pay you back right now. I've been carrying the money ever since the following day."

"Later. I'm glad you told me. I didn't notice the money missing for some time after you borrowed the car, and I couldn't find any way to ask. I'd begun to doubt I'd even put it there."

"You did, and I took it. Are we going to be cool?"

Mike nodded. "Neither of us said anything because we were afraid of damaging our friendship, and now it appears we both carried our separate burdens needlessly." He shrugged. "Okay, guys, let's play cards."

"Ned has the three of spades. Omar has the six of clubs. Paul has the jack of hearts. Dealer has the queen of hearts. Pass the bottle, and toss in your chip."

"What's jack of hearts?"

"Love. Or sex. An event you've never told any of us."

Paul sniffed. "I slept with Rachel once."

"What?"

Mike placed a hand on Ned's arm. "Let him talk."

"That's it. Long time ago. We were drinking. She was crying, and I held her and then. Then."

"Rachel never mentioned this to me."

"We were drinking. Afterwards, we agreed to pretend it never happened. A secret. No victim, no crime."

Mike cleared his throat. "Anybody need a break before I deal the next card? No? Okay. We're watching for the fourth and final jack, looking for a winner."

"What about the hole cards?"

"If I deal out the deck without finding the last jack, then we flip them over to see who has it. Otherwise, they're dead."

"I don't know where you find these games."

"I told you. Rachel." Mike proceeded to deal. "Ned has

the king of hearts. Omar has the king of diamonds. Paul has the jack of spades. Dealer has the king of spades."

Mike pushed the bottle towards Ned. "Drink."

The bottle went around the table. Chips clicked against those already there.

Paul stared at the jack of spades. "What's it mean?"

"A lie. Correct a lie you told us. Then gather your winnings."

Paul sniffed. "A lie. Okay, what the heck. We're all friends here. Water under the bridge is long gone."

"Go on."

"I didn't lie so much as leave out some parts."

"Who doesn't?"

"Right. Exactly. Have to make a long story short."

"You didn't want to drag it out."

"No, of course not."

"So tell us what really happened."

"Long time ago." Paul picked up the card. "I'd been drinking. Went over to her place to talk. Just needed someone to listen. Someone to care. Somehow things went wrong."

"Rachel."

"You all know her, know how she can be. I lost control."

Mike leaned forward. "You raped her."

"I raped her."

"And you never told anyone."

"Neither did she."

"Wrong. She told me." Mike turned to Ned. "She wanted my advice on how she should break it to you. She's tired of hiding the truth."

Ned stood. "You raped Rachel?"

Omar covered his ears, studied the cards on the table.
"It didn't mean anything."
"What?"
Mike pushed the pile of chips towards Paul.

Ned came around the table. "You and I are going to have a little talk."

Omar started. "Hey, there's two threes of clubs."

Mike pushed back his chair as Ned grabbed Paul's shirt. "I gambled that nothing odd would happen."

Ned pulled Paul to his feet and pushed him against the wall.

Mike leaned towards Omar. "This time, I'm not doing it alone. Rachel belongs to all of us."

Omar turned to see Paul's bloodied face and, with a deep sigh, dealt himself in.

Packy Run

Before Neil met me, he didn't know what a packy was. "Packy. A package store. A liquor store. Where we get our booze."

Before I met Neil, I didn't know what trouble was. "No one will ever know it was us. And even if they do, they won't press charges."

Classes accounted for fifteen hours a week, homework an additional five. I spent ten hours washing dishes in the cafeteria and probably another ten taking care of basic needs. That was forty hours out of a long and boring one hundred and sixty-eight, which left me with one hundred and twenty-eight hours to kill.

How much could I sleep? With Neil as a roommate, not much.

"No one will ever know it was us."

Sorry, Neil, but you're wrong. We're now on the surveillance tapes of at least a dozen liquor stores. Maybe the cops don't have our names yet, but that's only because this little spree of yours happened too fast.

I watched through the window of the packy, occasionally glancing into the rearview mirror to look for flashing lights.

Neil grabbed a brown paper bag from outstretched hands and dashed toward me, the gun gripped in his free hand.

Letting off the brake, I reversed in an arc so that the passenger door faced Neil. He yanked it open and jumped in: "Go, go, go."

I shifted into drive and hit the accelerator, banging left to get out of the parking lot and then right onto the street.

We squealed as we turned onto the entrance ramp, and then we were flying down the highway.

"Any problems?"

"Piece of cake. The clerk even said he'd throw in a flask of whiskey if I didn't kill him. As if I couldn't shoot him and take whatever I wanted."

I managed to keep my eyes on the road. "You wouldn't do that, would you?"

"Do what?"

"Shoot him."

"Heck, it's too late now. We'd have to get off at the next exit and turn around." He laughed.

I didn't. "The deal was no one got hurt."

"So long as they keep handing over the money, no one will."

My turn to go into the store was next. Then I'd ask Neil to count the money to see if he had enough. I wanted to call it quits before he did something stupid.

Neil had a weakness for betting on sporting events and a real strength for choosing losers. He borrowed money from the wrong people to pay back a different group of wrong people, and he lost that on a long shot.

Neil had twenty-four hours to raise twenty thousand dollars.

He pulled the flask of whiskey from the bag, used his thumb to spin the top off and send it flying against the windshield.

We'd known each other six weeks.

Neil leaned against his desk. "No one will ever know it was us. And even if they do, they won't press charges."

I sat up on my bed to take another sip of beer. "How do you figure that?"

"Who wants to admit they're grabbing quickies in the bushes behind the library? The flash will blind them, and by the time they pull on their clothes, we'll be just another pair of students sitting in a study carousel."

"Why do you want the pictures?"

"I don't. It's just the thrill of getting them."

"So why do you need me?"

"Lookout. Besides, you're my roommate. How could I not invite you on the adventure?"

I chugged the rest of beer, laid the empty on the pile. "Someone is going to take a swing at you."

"Let them try."

Neil tipped back the flask and then handed it towards me.

I shook my head. "Later. When we're back in the room."

"Can't promise there'll be any left."

Gripping the wheel, I forced myself to keep my eyes open despite the urge to make it all go away.

"The name's Neil, Neil Masterly." He tossed his bags onto the empty bed.

"Chris Robins, Comp Sci."

"What's that?"

"My major."

Neil snorted as he studied my side of the room. "I hope you're not a stuffed shirt geek pinhead."

"Actually, I'm Episcopalian."

"And what, pray tell, is that?"

There was something about Neil that just made me want to please him. "I don't know. I just thought it sounded good."

Neil slapped me on the shoulder. "You and me, we're going to go places before this semester is out."

A sign informed me it was ten miles to the next exit. I was chewing up the highway as if I could get ahead of myself somehow and avert the accident that seemed inevitable.

Six weeks I'd been skidding and gathering speed.

Neil and I took pictures of horny college students. Then we started tapping on people's windows with a long pole until someone woke up and parted the curtains. Then we let air out of tires, ten to twenty cars at a time, skipping from lot to lot.

I never enjoyed his adventures as much as he did, but I went along because it seemed the thing to do.

No one ever told me how easily a line could be crossed, how quickly a line moved as though it had a life of its own.

Yesterday, Neil handed me a beer and said he needed my help. Then he told me about the gambling and the debt he'd racked up. When did he find the time?

Neil waggled the flask of whiskey. "Last chance."

I took a hit before handing the bottle back.

"My grandmother could drink you under the table."

"Here's the exit." I slid off the highway and followed the ramp down to the split. Left or right? Which way to the nearest packy?

On a whim, I turned right.

Neil had only mentioned his family once before. He was changing into a dark shirt for some night work when I saw a ragged scar running down his arm.

"What happened?"

"My mom came at me with a pair of scissors to keep me from beating up my old man after I learned he raped my kid sister."

In seventh grade I was grounded for a weekend when I received a C on a math exam. I was crushed.

"Families. Aren't you glad we're finally on our own?"

Ahead I saw the bright neons that advertised booze.

Neil tossed the empty flask out the window and now we could add littering to charges of armed robbery.

As soon as I stopped the car, he opened his door.

I grabbed his arm. "It's my turn."

Neil shook his head and removed my hand. "I have a feeling about this one."

"What the hell is that supposed mean?"

Neil stared out the windshield and sighed. "When I was your age, I killed my first man."

"What are you talking about? You are my age."

When he finally turned to face me, his eyes were empty, rimmed with red. "Don't try to stop me."

"Let's go home."

"Why?" Neil rolled out of the car and ran towards the package store before I could formulate a response never mind tackle him.

Through the glass door I watched Neil show the gun to the man behind the counter. *Please, God, don't let him pull the trigger.*

I slipped the phone from my pocket, thumbed through the menus until I reached Contacts and found 911. My thumb trembled as I held it over the dial button.

Neil took a brown paper bag from the man.

Did the clerk have family, a wife and kids? Were his parents still alive? Was he a good friend?

Neil waggled his gun.

Did the clerk volunteer to help the handicapped? Was he quick with a joke, a helping hand? Was he well-loved and much-liked?

Neil laughed.

Maybe, just maybe, the clerk was scum of the earth.

My thumb rested on the button.

Neil backed away from the counter and turned to face me.

I heard myself exhale.

Neil dashed toward me, eyes wide and mouth open as if he was trying to scream.

I jammed the phone back in my pocket before he had a chance to see it and ask for an explanation.

Neil's outstretched hand touched the door handle.

I jumped at a loud boom, and Neil was pressed up against the glass like one of those suction cups, his cheek forming a three-quarter moon.

The door in front of him starred at the impact, and through the cracks, I could see the blood on his shirt.

Neil dropped to the floor, one hand raised and held against the glass as if he was waiting for me to lay my hand on the other side in some kind of sentimental gesture.

I had to thumb through Contacts three times before I could read 911 through the tears. I pressed the button.

"Nine one one. Your call is being recorded."

All I could do was cry.

Pipe Dreams

Although Lieutenant Brant was already sitting at the corner booth when I entered the diner, I still stopped at the counter to place my order before joining him.

"Glad you could make it, Eldridge."

"I'm glad you asked to meet where we could get a decent cup of coffee. I have recurring nightmares about the sludge you serve me in your office."

"I thought you'd rather hear what I had to say somewhere other than downtown."

"Hear what?"

He laid his arms on the table. "First of all, it's not free. I need your help."

I thanked Zetra for the coffee, waited for her to leave before I used a napkin to clean what she'd spilled. "Is it work-related or something personal?"

The Lieutenant sighed. "I'm investigating another impossible crime."

I laughed. "Didn't I already solve one of those for you?"

"Yes, and I fixed Emily's ticket so your daughter wouldn't see her insurance rates skyrocket. We're even."

I sipped my coffee, watched him over the rim. "You seem a little touchy."

He sighed. "Yeah, well, this isn't easy."

"Take your time."

"We'll start with my problem. Then we'll get to yours."

The Lieutenant took a deep breath. "A guy got himself killed over on Windsor Heights. The house is a reproduction of some famous Mexican villa, adobe construction, tile roof, no screens on the windows. The lot is surrounded by a six-foot stone wall with a locked gate in front."

"Thinking of a second career as a real estate agent?"

The Lieutenant scowled. "Arthur Pelham was killed by a poisoned dart. He must have heard something while he was sitting at his desk because he crossed to the window and ... pow."

"It was probably more like a pfft."

He ignored my joke. "We found the blow pipe inside the wall. The shooter probably dropped it by mistake."

I took another sip of coffee. "Have you found any witnesses?"

"Nobody saw, heard, or smelled anything."

"You asked about smell?"

The Lieutenant finally smiled, if ruefully. "It's the poisoned dart. Wouldn't a tribal medicine man decked out with war-paint and feathers have built a fire to dance around first?"

"That's a question for the profiling unit at the FBI." I motioned to Zetra for a refill. "So why did you call this an impossible crime? Maybe the weapon is a little esoteric, but I imagine any nonsmoker can fire one."

"There's a catch."

"Isn't there always."

"The window that the dart was shot through, it was closed."

"Wind?"

The Lieutenant shook his head. "You really have to

work to open and close those windows. I mean tug. According to the housekeeper, Pelham kept the windows open for the air."

"Who discovered the body?"

"Patrol officer. Neighbor called the police when Pelham didn't show up for their daily game of chess and didn't answer his telephone."

Zetra stopped by to top off my coffee.

I turned to the Lieutenant. "Aren't you having anything?"

He shook his head. "My stomach is bothering me."

"Warm milk?"

"Not unless you want me to puke."

I smiled up at Zetra. "That will be all."

I took notes as the Lieutenant gave me a rundown on his suspects. Each had an alibi, none ironclad.

"How much leeway on the time of death?"

"Pelham busted his watch on the desk when he fell."

My expression must have spoken volumes because he quickly continued, "The ME says it can't be more than an hour off, according to core body temp."

"Do I have access to the property?"

"Sure. But I made you copies of the crime scene photos."

I smiled. "Because you'd rather not have the media notice me going into the house."

The Lieutenant winced. "Bringing in a PI isn't quite the same as hiring a psychic, but they'd hang me just as high."

"Okay, I'll work your impossible crime. Now, what's this thing I need to hear?"

The Lieutenant looked down at his hands, bobbed his Adam's apple a few times. "We've been keeping an eye on a dealer, building a case. We've got Emily on tape."

"My Emily?"

He nodded. "Your daughter bought a bag of marijuana."

I didn't know what to say. How much did she use that she knew a dealer? I saw her every weekend. How could I have missed the signs? There had to be a mistake. "Are you sure?"

The Lieutenant grimaced and put his hand to his chest. "I've had heartburn ever since I realized I needed to let you know."

"How long?"

"A week. Then the murder came up and gave me an angle. I pulled the tape." He slipped a brown paper bag onto the table. "The crime scene photos are in there too. What are you going to tell your ex?"

"I don't know." The ugliness of the divorce behind us, we managed to remain friendly enough to raise a teenage girl between us.

"You can't keep your ex in the dark. Emily lives with her five days out of seven."

"Maybe it was a one-time thing."

The Lieutenant's face said it all. Someone who wanted to experiment did so with a friend, not a dealer.

"Right."

He pulled himself out of the booth. "You know where to find me."

"Sure." I glanced at the paper bag, pushed it away. I'd always assumed she would come to me about something like this. Wasn't I her friend as well as her father? Apparently, I wasn't much of either.

Nursing the coffee, I reviewed the last few weekends to

see if I had missed some telltale clue. Perhaps I was blind to Emily's problems because she was my daughter, and I was a private investigator who saved other people's daughters.

Leaving money on the table, I left the diner and climbed into my car, the brown bag on my lap. I just sat there, staring off into space.

I'd probably be there still, except that I slammed my brake when the car next to me slowly reversed. I laughed at my mistake. At least the illusion was enough to disrupt my funk. I had an impossible crime to solve.

I opened the bag and ignored the tape, pulling out the photographs. The lieutenant had given me everything, even a shot of the photographer's shoe and a busy blur that almost made me dizzy just looking at it.

Among the better attempts at photography, there were four establishing shots of the room, one from each corner.

The desk was located in the center of the room, facing the door, back to the window.

The chair was lying on its side, and various office supplies littered the floor. Pelham was between the desk and the window, scrunched up on the rug as though he was trying to eat his way through.

There were close-ups of the body, the desk, and the window. Nothing jingled my bell.

Outside, there were photographs of the tree overhanging the wall, a series focusing on the murder weapon, and a shot that baffled me no matter which way I turned it.

I didn't know who was shooting the crime scene photos these days, but I wouldn't be surprised to discover he shared the same dealer as Emily.

Just what the heck was my daughter thinking?

I laid the crime scene photos on the dashboard.

Was this about the Correia boy? I testified against his father, so Emily punished me by getting involved with drugs?

No. Emily didn't stoop to mind games, and besides, she'd been brutally honest with me about her feelings before, during, and after the trial.

Perhaps she was going through a stage. Divorce could be hard on kids, and I knew she was overwhelmed by the task of deciding on her future.

Actually, for all I knew, Brant had misidentified her, and now I was grasping at straws.

I moved the crime scene photos to the passenger seat and started the engine. First I'd solve the Lieutenant's impossible crime. Then I'd try to untangle my own mess.

It must have been tough for him, informing me that I didn't know what was happening under my own roof. I was surprised he entrusted his murder case to a PI who couldn't see his hand in front of his face.

The Lieutenant had given me three names. Each of the people had motive. None appeared to have means. Opportunity was up for grabs.

I took a left onto Manchester.

Pelham's daughter ran a mystery bookstore located just outside the fringes of nearly almost downtown. I didn't imagine she saw much foot traffic.

There was a single parking space in front of Missing Persons. It was empty until I pulled in.

I entered the bookstore, waited for the chimes to bring Sandy to the counter from the back room. "Do you have any John Dickson Carr?"

"Not in stock."

"Edward Hoch?"

"Sorry." Her left eyebrow twitched when I pronounced his name correctly to rhyme with coke.

"Impossible crimes are sort of a hobby with me."

Sandy smiled. "The puzzle does gladden the intellect."

"I hear you've had some experience."

"Whatever do you mean?"

"Your father."

She drew in a slow breath. "Are you with the police?"

"I'm a private detective." I placed my card on the counter next to a pile of bookmarks. "The name's Eldridge."

"Why the ploy?"

"I've never been good at introductions." I glanced around the bookstore. "Is this a good time to talk?"

"I already told the police everything I know, which isn't much. We were never close. I doubt I've spoken to him once in the last ten years."

"You're in the will."

She shrugged. "He managed to appease his conscience in such a way that he wouldn't live to see the expense."

"That's clever."

"He was a clever man."

"I meant your turn of phrase."

"One can't help but be educated by what one reads."

"That's where I came in, asking about books concerning impossible crimes."

"Yes." She smiled. "Are you hoping I'll confess to the murder?"

"That would make my life easier."

"It would also make me a liar."

Unable to stop myself from laughing aloud, I held up my hands. "You win. Assuming you've learned something from all your reading, who do you think killed Pelham?"

"I didn't know him well enough to know his enemies. In fiction, the least likely suspect is often guilty. In real life, isn't it just the opposite?"

"Sometimes."

Sandy picked up my card. "I'll call you if his ghost comes to me with an accusation."

"Or, after the case is over, to invite me to dinner."

She held my gaze. "And if I'm the one you put away?"

"A very late dinner."

She smiled. "You'd better get cracking."

Since I couldn't think of a comeback quickly enough, I left Sandy with the last word. Driving towards the next name on the list, I wondered why I had allowed myself to flirt.

Of course I had the answer to that before I even finished asking the question. A new relationship would increase my obligations and responsibilities, shrinking the size of the pie labeled Emily.

How did I miss the smell of marijuana, the red eyes, the giggles? Later, I'd beat myself up later.

The second suspect was his housekeeper. Motive was slight. She admitted to sleeping with him and that he wanted to end the relationship. How scorned could she be, if she continued to work for him?

According to the Lieutenant, for the next several hours I should be able to find her over on Piedmont, since she cleaned houses in rigid half-day blocks.

I parked in front of 72 Piedmont, a large Georgian that dwarfed the low-end Toyota in the driveway, and sneaked a peek through the vehicle's windows as I passed. The car was spotless.

I brushed off the pang of shoemaker's guilt.

At the front door, I pressed the lighted button and listened to the dulcimer tones that escaped from an open window.

Thirty seconds later, a woman answered the door. "Can I help you?"

"Gail Landers?"

She blinked. "Yes. How did you ..."

"I'm a private detective investigating the murder of Arthur Pelham. Lieutenant Brant told me where I could find you."

Gail glanced at her watch. "You know I'm working."

"Just a few minutes of your time is all I need."

She paused. "We can talk while I scrub the toilet."

"Just so long as you don't vacuum." She didn't laugh, but then she'd already turned away to lead me into the house, so perhaps she didn't hear what I said.

Inside, the place was even more impressive than the outside had prepared me to believe.

Gail walked quickly, and I almost lost her at an intersection. She was pulling on thick plastic gloves when I found her in the bathroom.

I whistled. "This is one big bathroom."

"The larger the bathroom, the easier it is to clean."

"What's Pelham's bathroom like?"

Gail lifted the toilet seat and sprayed all surfaces with some noxious chemical. I could feel my nostril hairs vibrate before entering their death throes.

"Small and difficult." She lifted a two-headed brush from a tool chest on the floor and began scrubbing, switching back and forth between the bristle and the sponge.

"Who do you think killed him?"

"His affairs were none of my concern."

"One was."

There was a slight break in her perfect stroke. "That is history."

"So is Pelham. Why did you continue to work for him?"

"I needed the money."

My toilet hadn't been as clean when new. "I imagine a good housekeeper is in demand."

"Finding a client takes time. I couldn't afford to have an open slot right now."

"Why right now?"

She stopped, took a deep breath which must have frosted her lungs. "If I answer your question, will you leave me to finish my work in peace?"

"Certainly." After all, I had her schedule.

"I need to earn as much as I can now, because I'll have to cut back on my hours once I have the baby."

"Is Pelham the father?"

"He was."

I left my card on the toolbox and eventually found my way out of the house.

Did the pregnancy give Gail more motive or less? Remembering the state of my apartment, could I afford her rates?

Was parenthood ever as simple as we imagined?

Chuck Kutner was Pelham's old business partner. He didn't keep regular hours anywhere and didn't answer any of the telephone numbers I'd been given by the Lieutenant.

Three years after selling their business, the two men

were still claiming the other cooked the books and skimmed profits. With Pelham dead, Chuck wouldn't have to defend himself against allegations of embezzlement, though he may have traded that for a charge of first-degree murder.

Emily had to realize that an arrest would haunt her forever.

College admission departments took a dim view of court-ordered community service, and employers almost always asked about criminal records. Did the process of mapping her future so freak her out that Emily was trying to sabotage her efforts?

I forced the thoughts from my head so I could focus on the issue at hand. The Lieutenant told me that Chuck was a big darts player, so I started checking the taverns.

Twenty minutes later, a bartender pointed him out.

"Chuck Kutner?"

He turned his head but kept his eyes on his opponent's tosses. "Yeah."

I explained why I was there.

Chuck smiled, probably more at his opponent's inability to score than at the pleasure of my company.

He spoke out of the corner of his mouth. "Give me five minutes."

Chuck licked his fingers as he approached the line. I withdrew to the bar and asked for a soda and lemon.

The bartender handed me my drink. "You here to play Chuck?"

"In a way."

"I won't be able to start you a tab, then."

I placed a five on the bar, turned to watch my suspect.

Chuck played a mean game of cricket. Not two minutes

went by before he joined me, thumbing a sheaf of bills. "I don't suppose you're a dart man."

"Not against you, I'm not."

He laughed, ordered a beer.

Chuck folded the winnings into his shirt pocket and gave me his full attention. "So what do you want to know?"

"Someone painted a bulls-eye on Pelham. What do you make of that?"

"We had our difficulties." Chuck took a sip of his beer. "Pelham wasn't an easy man. We fought the entire time we worked together and ever since. Some people are like that. They rub you the wrong way and do it on purpose."

"So you're not surprised someone killed him."

"Surprised? Yes. I had more reason than most to hate Pelham, but hate doesn't necessarily translate to murder. I projected his face onto whatever spot I wanted to hit. Now that Pelham's gone, I'm going to need to find a new nemesis, or I'm through."

"You know he was killed by a poisoned dart."

Chuck sniffed. "And maybe if he lived until next month he'd be run down by a Dodge Dart. Big deal."

"When was the last time you talked to him?"

"Face to face? Maybe a month and a half. The only friends we had in common were the lawyers."

I nodded toward the dartboard. "Thanks for the demonstration."

"Any time."

As I left the bar I turned on my phone and saw that I had a message. I called Emily back from the car.

"What's up?"

"Can we get together and talk?"

"Sure. Where and when?"

"I'm at work right now, but it's slow, and they're letting me go home early."

"I'll pick you up in front of the west entrance in fifteen."

"Great."

I started the car.

Emily was a Purchasing Assistant at Oddz N Endz, one of perhaps a dozen accessory stores at the mall.

She knew more about hair ornamentation than anyone should have to. Or perhaps that was only me talking. I smiled as I pictured Emily rolling her eyes at her Daddy so hopelessly out of touch.

My warm feeling faded when I remembered just how out of touch I was. If Emily wanted to talk about something besides her drug use, how did I broach the subject?

I could ask three perfect strangers whether they were guilty of murder, but I didn't want to hear my daughter say she was naughty.

To distract myself from the coming conversation, I mulled over the three suspects. Perhaps the key to this case was the bizarre manner in which Pelham was killed. Solve the puzzle, and win a confession.

Say the window was open when the dart was fired. Pelham could have taken the shot, closed the window to protect himself from a second, and then fallen to the floor. Unless the poison was instantaneous, facing meant nothing.

The thing was, I couldn't picture any of the suspects up in that tree, extending a blowpipe over the wall, making a sound to catch Pelham's attention and draw him towards the open window.

I entered the mall parking lot and made my way to the west entrance.

Why depend on such a complicated approach? Pelham might have turned his head and seen the killer while still at his desk. Then all he needed to do was stand and step aside. A dart wasn't going through thick, adobe walls.

I slowed as I reached the entrance and saw Emily disengage from the group standing there. Stopping, I unlocked the passenger door.

Emily slid into the seat and pecked me on the cheek.

Her eyes appeared normal and she wasn't covered with crumbs. On the other hand, she had paper clips hanging from her ears. "Anywhere in particular you want to go?"

She shook her head. "Just around. Mom's picking me up in half an hour. My car's in the shop."

"I can bring you home."

Emily bit her lip. "Mom can't know we talked."

"Okay. I'll just circle the mall then. The size of this lot, it may take twenty minutes to complete the loop."

Turning to the window, Emily sighed. "This isn't easy."

"Lieutenant Brant said the same thing earlier today. I'll tell you what I told him: take your time."

"I don't know if I should. She asked me not to."

"She?"

"Mom."

"Mom?"

Emily nodded. "Mom found a lump. They operated, discovered more traces. Now she's on chemo."

I slowed, turned into an empty slot and killed the engine. "Are you saying she has cancer?"

Emily covered her face. "The prognosis is good. No one but me even knows."

Shifting in my seat, I pulled Emily into my arms. "I'm sorry."

"It's not fair."

"Why is she keeping it a secret?"

"You know Mom."

I did. And I could understand her point of view. Heck, if I had cancer, I wouldn't even let myself know. "You say the doctors are hopeful?"

"Very." Her voice was muffled by our embrace. Emily sat up and wiped her eyes. "I'm probably a fool for even mentioning it to you. Mom wouldn't like it."

"I'm your father."

Emily made a brave attempt at a smile. "It's helped just to talk." She sniffed. "You better take me back. Now I need to freshen up so Mom doesn't know I was crying."

"How's Mom reacting to the chemo?"

"It makes her sick. Believe it or not, I've been buying her marijuana."

"Does it help?"

"Mostly."

I started the engine and turned the car around. I'd been prepared to convince Emily to enter a drug rehab program, and here she was trying to help her Mom cope with the side effects of cancer treatment. "The dealer you've been buying from is under police surveillance."

"You're joking."

"I'll talk to the Lieutenant, work something out, find you a safer source."

"Thanks, Daddy."

"You, ah, haven't tried any yourself, have you?"

"No. I heard pot interferes with how heroin is metabolized." Emily laughed before I had a chance to have a heart attack. "Gotcha."

I stopped in front of the west entrance. "You did."

Emily pecked me on the cheek again before leaving.

My ex and I had been married fifteen years. She never even got the flu. Colds that laid me out inconvenienced her for a few hours. I only hoped the doctors knew what they were doing.

Someone behind me honked, and I suddenly realized I'd been sitting there so long Emily was no longer in sight. Waving in the rearview mirror, I drove back to the diner to re-caffeinate.

I brought the brown paper bag in with me, dumped the tape into the trash on my way to a booth where I spread out the crime scene photos.

I examined them again, one at a time.

Nothing had changed except for me. I now saw what I missed before, and I knew why the murderer used such an arcane method.

I tested my theory, tried to find holes. Believing myself more right by the minute, I called Brant.

"So who's the killer?"

"Gail Landers, the housekeeper. If you paid any attention to the crime scene photos, you would have noticed paper clips and rubber bands under the desk. You might even have asked yourself why."

"Why?"

"She rigged the dart to shoot Pelham when he opened his middle drawer. The blowpipe in the yard was a red herring. It was just her bad luck that he closed the window the day of the murder."

"What's her motive?"

"Love. Do you have the lab results yet on the poison?"

"They're working on it."

"Don't be surprised if it's a combination of industrial strength cleaning agents." I took a deep breath. "And I talked with Emily. She's okay. I'll explain more later."

"Good work. Buy yourself a coffee."

"Consider it done."

After signaling Zetra for a coffee, I slid the crime scene photos together and returned them to the bag.

Puzzling

There was only one way to do a puzzle in the Magri house.

First, his mother stared at the cover of the box for five minutes before making Robert stare at it for another five.

Today, he could barely see the glossy image through the tears that kept welling up.

Second, the box was opened, and the pieces were lifted out one by one. Edge pieces were placed in the middle of the table, face up, with the straight side to the left. Corner pieces were placed below the grid of edge pieces. Interior pieces were placed, face up, on the far end of the table grouped according to color, pattern, or guiding principle.

Third, the corner pieces were examined and placed in their respective corners, the correct distance apart.

Robert could recite the drill in his sleep, but then, he should be able to after some twenty odd years of it. Mother knew the best way to do a puzzle. She knew the best way to do everything, the best thing for everyone. There was no point in arguing with her.

Fourth, the edge pieces were slowly fitted together until the frame of the puzzle was complete.

Robert sat stiffly while his mother worked the bottom side of the puzzle, her hands sure and quick.

She spoke without looking at him, "You're not being much help today, Robert."

"Sorry. I'm thinking about the funeral tomorrow."

"Work on the puzzle. It will free your mind."

Picking up an edge piece, Robert tried to forget that his beloved Jewel was dead, tried to lose himself in the utterly pointless mystery of the jigsaw.

Fifth, the grouped pieces would be assembled and the sections carefully lifted and situated in their approximate resting place within the frame.

Sixth, the last connecting pieces would be used to pull everything together.

Seventh, his mother would stand and stare, beaming, at the finished product.

Robert rotated the cardboard piece as though he was trying to imagine where it might fit, but in reality, he only saw Jewel's face, still and paler than usual. His Jewel had been poisoned, taken away from him.

Tonight was the viewing, and his mother refused to vary from the routine of the Saturday evening puzzle.

Conscious that his mother was waiting for him to do his part, Robert shook himself and examined the puzzle piece.

A path was leading off the left side; there was a splash of reds along the bottom of the piece signifying the flowerbed; the nub at the top of the piece turned green, which was the bottom of the hedge. There was little, if any, doubt where the piece fit.

Robert lifted the piece closer. There on the path ... it almost looked like a knife. "Can I see the cover again?"

His mother smiled and passed him the box top.

There was the path leading off the left side of the puzzle, but there was no sign of a knife.

Robert felt a moment's dizziness, and then it was gone.

The puzzle was a print of an oil painting. What he thought had been a knife must simply have been brush strokes used to darken the path.

Handing the box back to his mother, Robert placed the edge piece approximately where it would eventually lie.

Jewel's father swore that he hadn't killed her, that he had never seen the poison found under the bathroom sink. He said he could never have killed his daughter, and Robert believed him, even if the police didn't.

Her father had no motive. The two of them had a completely normal father-daughter relationship, untainted by thoughts of homicide. Jewel's father had been happy that she and Robert were talking marriage. Robert had experienced him as supportive and kind.

Robert's mother interrupted his thoughts to suggest that Robert work one of the groups at the other end of the table. "I'll finish the frame myself."

His mother must have seen the knife on that edge piece and wanted to keep him far away from it. She was the type of person who thought she always knew what was best. She enjoyed controlling him like some kind of mindless puppet.

Robert picked at the pieces in the group nearest to him. The patterns of green with patches of red seemed to represent the series of rose bushes from the bottom right part of the puzzle. Here were two pieces that fit together, and there was a third. Working on the puzzle did free up the mind, did give the subconscious free rein to search for patterns.

Connections became apparent that were otherwise invisible.

Robert saw a human leg partially hidden by the bush.

He quickly fitted together another pair of pieces and then found the piece that bridged the two groups. Another four pieces, and the picture was plain: there was a body lying behind the rose bushes.

It was his mother who was dead this time. He could see the blood spilled by the knife dropped on the path. All his life he had imagined being free of her.

Robert wondered if his mother would notice the body that didn't appear on the box cover and realized that she wouldn't. She wasn't the type to be bothered by a guilty conscience, proud of every horrible thing she had ever done, firmly believing she had been right to do it.

She looked up at him. "Don't rest on your laurels. There's still a long way to go."

Robert started looking through a fresh group of pieces, all swirling fogs of blue and white. These were the sky, and there was a lot of it.

The sky was often the hardest part of any puzzle. Instead of colors, there were shades; instead of pattern, there was dissolution. The sky saw everything and gave nothing back.

On the other hand, it didn't poison the only girl you'd ever loved just so you wouldn't leave.

Robert felt his pulse race. Now he knew why his mother had decided to visit the future in-laws. At the time, Robert thought she was merely trying to scare them off. He should have guessed that she'd never leave something so important to chance.

As if of its own volition, his right finger traced the dead body that only he saw.

She'd killed the love of his life, his only hope for a life. Somehow, left alone in the next-door neighbor's kitchen, she must have added poison to the soda that Jewel drank, probably telling herself that she was acting in Robert's best interest.

No one suspected her. Who, not knowing her, would? A mother should be glad of a son's happiness. Why expect anything else?

Robert ran his eyes over the puzzle, grateful, for once, that she forced him to do this thing tonight of all nights. He wouldn't have known what she'd done otherwise, wouldn't know what to do.

His father had never helped with puzzles when he still lived here, he drew the line at that. He hadn't understood that puzzles were more than printed pieces of cardboard.

Puzzles were a way of re-seeing reality.

Robert was beginning to grasp the power and magic of this thing that was no mere entertainment no matter how much his mother corrupted and cheapened it with her ploys for control.

For the first time since he was struck down by the news, Robert felt truly alive. He had tapped into something mystical tonight.

When Pasteur discovered penicillin, when Einstein discovered relativity, when Beethoven discovered his Fifth Symphony, they weren't producing something from nothing. They were using their minds and souls to find the patterns in the pieces that nature had provided.

Robert wiped the sweat from his forehead and began fitting the sky together before his mother noticed that he was just sitting again.

Could Jewel's father prove that he was innocent? Could the evidence be spun like a knife to point at Robert's mother? No, she was too smart for that. She was the master puppeteer.

There was only one option left to him, an option laid out before him in living color. His mother must die for her crime.

Robert focused on working the puzzle again, concentrated on the empty sky so that he could ignore the body hidden beneath the rose bush.

First, they would finish the puzzle. He would give his mother that last satisfaction.

Then, while she was basking in her glory, he would retrieve a knife from the kitchen and do what he wished he had done any of a million previous times.

Robert bit back a sob.

If only he had, Jewel would still be alive. They'd be sitting on the couch laughing, imagining their future together.

Instead, he was facing a life alone, racking his brains for the nearest set of rose bushes where he would bury the remains of his past.

Raising the Bar

How long would it have taken me to hammer in that nail? Five minutes, if I'd bothered to look for a hammer? Thirty seconds, if I'd simply slipped off a high-heeled shoe and aimed carefully?

That nail had been protruding from the wall since the day I moved into the apartment. Dozens of times I thought I should do something about it.

I never did.

Frank Junior stayed with my Ma while I went to work. He filled the hole his grandfather left, and she saved me the worry and expense of pre-school childcare. None of us were particularly happy with the arrangement.

"Hi, Ma."

Frank Junior looked up from his drawing, and I had to stop myself from gasping, even now. "Mama."

I leaned over the kitchen table and kissed him, my little angel boy. "Hi, Sweetie. Were you good for Grandma?"

"He was excellent."

My mother was standing at the stove, stirring a pot of something that smelled like tepid water, not quite close enough to Frank Junior for my comfort, but who was I to talk?

"What did the two of you do today?"

"Frank drew with his crayons."

I lifted him into my arms and snuggled against his

neck. "The entire time?"

"He's very talented."

"Yes, you are. You draw very well."

"Red."

"Did you draw pictures with your red crayon?"

"Blue."

"And your blue crayon? Wow." I could look at his face without wincing, but I wondered sometimes if he saw the anguish in my eyes. That nail had ripped ...

"He had some apple sauce about an hour ago."

"Did you give him the sugar-free kind?"

"I gave him what was on sale."

My mother never blamed me. No one did. Accidents happened every single day. Children his age were always getting hurt one way or another. It was nobody's fault. There, but for the grace of God, go I.

"The sales quarter ends this week. I probably have to work late tomorrow. If not, the next day." I jostled Frank Junior until he giggled.

"It's no trouble."

"Good. I'll call once I know for certain."

"The number hasn't changed in forty-seven years." Ma wasn't the type to make me feel guilty. She didn't evoke much feeling at all.

"Well, I have to get my darling prince home so I can fill," tickle, tickle, "his ticklish belly."

Frank Junior was laughing as we left the kitchen. My mother was stirring.

I still had nightmares that people took Frank Junior away from me because I was an unfit mother. My son was scarred, disfigured for life, because I had been too lazy to hammer in one lone nail.

Plastic things were stuck in unused outlets. Cords were taped down. Drawers were fastened, and poisons were hidden, and I served milk with every meal.

He was new to running, and he slipped. He fell in the worst possible direction towards the object I warned him never to touch.

Frank Junior sat in the car seat waiting for me to finish securing his belt. He knew that as soon as I was done, he'd get a cracker for the ride home.

"Here you go, Honey."

"Crack."

I locked the door before swinging it closed and stared at my mother's house before climbing behind the wheel. I didn't know what I'd do without her.

"Did you have fun today, Sweetie?"

"Crack."

"Yes, you have a cracker."

I started the car and headed home.

A therapist came and sat with me one day at the hospital, asking questions to see how I was coping. She only managed to rouse me when she suggested I might be angry with Frank Junior for getting hurt.

"He didn't do anything wrong. He didn't disobey me, break any rules. He was running. We were playing a game."

"You can't blame yourself."

"I certainly can't shift the blame to him."

She talked with me another ten minutes, but I never saw her again. I wasn't sure whether she thought I was bearing up nicely or beyond human help.

Many people in my position would have prayed. My mother would have. She did. I'd lived without faith for too long to find comfort in running back to the God of my youth. Besides, Frank Junior was the victim, not me.

I put on a happy face when he was awake, and I quietly wept as soon as his breath evened out and slowed.

"Crack."

"Good cracker?"

Frank Junior nodded in the rearview mirror.

"We're almost home, Honey."

Some days, I thought about calling that therapist.

But what if my feelings weren't normal? What if I was some kind of monster? What if I was unfit?

She'd nod and take notes, and then the people would come and take Frank Junior away from me.

It was better to say nothing.

Upstairs, the light on the answering machine was blinking.

"It's me. I'll be out of town for the next month so the check will be a little late. Thanks."

Thanks for what? For being understanding? For not calling the cops? For loaning him the money so he could take some floozy to the beach?

I put Frank Junior in his highchair and rolled three trucks across the recessed tray. "Broom, broom."

"Tra."

"Mommy is going to make supper while you play with your trucks."

"Tra."

The nail incident did change me, changed me in a way I never would have expected. I had hurt my baby — inadvertently, but hurt him nonetheless. I had raised the bar of what was acceptable.

Since that day, I yelled at him more. What was

shouting compared to what I'd allowed to happen?

Since that day, and for the first time, I imagined striking him when he didn't listen, when he fought me during changing, when he acted out the way children do. After all, look at what I'd already done.

These were the thoughts I was afraid of sharing.

Maybe they were normal, and the therapist could reassure me.

Maybe they weren't.

I forked the hot dog out of the boiling water onto a plate, turned off the burner, and moved the pot to the sink.

What happened, happened. There was no way of changing that, no way of going back. But what was I capable of now? How had the accident twisted my sense of right and wrong?

"Okay, Sweetie, would you like pea jar or carrot jar?"

"Jaw."

I took a jar of peas down from the cupboard and emptied a third into a plastic bowl. Holding the hot dog with the fork, I sliced it in half down the middle and then chopped off thin chunks. Finally I poured milk into a sippy cup. "All ready."

"Red."

Sitting in front of Frank Junior, I smiled. "Are you hungry?"

He nodded and handed me a truck.

"Thank you. Have to pick up." I put the trucks on the table and slipped the bib over his head. I'd take care of myself later. I didn't want to lose a second of available focusing. "Time to eat. Hot dog and peas and milk."

"Mill."

I spooned him some peas. "Hot dog needs to cool

down."

"Dow."

He leaned forward to suck more pea off the spoon.

What if I stopped giving him vegetables? It certainly wasn't a crime, but how much damage would I do to his developing body? What if I fed him junk around the clock?

What if I stunted his growth or made him obese?

As it was, I was probably missing some significant vitamin or mineral, the deficiency cursing him to future health problems. He could thank me then for my weak knowledge of basic nutrition.

He could thank me for my inattention to detail.

I tested a bit of hot dog against my lips.

"Dow."

"Yes, it's cooling down. Almost. Drink some milk."

I understood one thing about my feelings. Frank Junior was a daily reminder of my mistake. Every time I gazed at his sweet and tender face I was slapped by the reality of that nail.

How long would it have taken me?

Hot dogs were a known choking hazard. If I didn't cut the pieces small enough, if I urged him to stuff too many into his mouth, I might be excused from forever seeing the unmistakable evidence of my negligence, excused from being the chief witness against myself.

These things happened.

If Frank Junior died tonight, I would no longer have to worry about how the scars would affect him at sixteen, twenty-four, seventy. I would not have to question, at every juncture of his life, how that nail might have impacted the results.

Of course, the price was impossibly high.

I fed Frank Junior a piece of hot dog after checking the temperature once more.

"Dow."

"Yes, cooled down."

I would bear the guilt because I was his mother, and I loved him. I would resist the temptation of anger, of escape, and I would cope the best that I could.

After all, why should I take my frustrations out on my baby?

Frank Senior would be away from his house for a month.

Rousted

I was still three blowjobs short of rent when I was rousted and brought downtown. Then that fat pig Devans tossed a Polaroid in front of me, and I didn't look away quickly enough.

"Do you recognize him?"

"A face would help."

Devans roared. "That's a good one. A face would help." He leaned closer, bringing the smell of sausage along. "Actually, I'm surprised you even notice faces, your line of work. Try again."

Picking up the photograph, I kept my eyes on a button that almost escaped the frame. "This isn't even in focus."

Devans sighed, sat back in his chair until it creaked. "Photographer's first day. He cried while he took the picture, and then he threw up."

The button was nothing special, the usual invisible white piece of plastic. "Why would I know this guy?"

"He was found shot to death at the Atlantic Motel, one of your stomping grounds."

I returned the photograph to the desk. "Lots of girls work there."

"And we're talking to lots of girls. It's a shitty day all around."

"Thanks for the compliment."

A crease appeared in his forehead. "Just answer the

question."

"Maybe I've seen him around. It's hard to say, you know?" My heel caught on the bottom of the metal desk as I crossed my legs. "Do you have a name for him?"

"Why? Do many of your customers tell you their name?"

"Yeah, but the funny thing is, most of them are named John."

Devans froze, trembled, then exploded into laughter, bits of stuff flying out of his mouth. "Most of them are named John? That is fucking hilarious."

"It's nice when you can bring a sense of humor to your job."

That cracked him up even more. He might never have caught his breath, but a junkie chained to a desk on the other side of the room started screaming. Devans threw him a nasty look. "Maybe you can't ID the stiff, but did you notice any new blood today?"

"There's always new girls. The life is a dream for many."

Devans tipped his chair back, crossed his arms behind his head so that I could appreciate his underarm stains. "I'm thinking the wife."

"You lost me." I glanced over his shoulder to the clock on the wall. The landlord wanted the rent in two hours, or me and my little girl were on the street.

"Our friend there was popped with his own gun, and it wasn't no suicide shot. My gut tells me the wife did it. She tarted herself up, played the whore, and killed the cheating bastard."

"That's why you asked me about new blood."

"Hey, I'm the Sherlock Holmes around here, but yeah. I

want to know who this guy was seen with."

"I couldn't swear I saw him at all."

Devans tipped forward again. "I'm not looking for an expert witness. A defense lawyer would discredit your testimony with a single question. I'm just looking for pointers."

I paused, weighed my words, how far I should take this. Time was running out. "Okay, I did see someone new. She stood back, didn't approach anybody."

"Did you see her with him?" Devans nodded toward the picture.

"Like I told you before, I don't know if I saw him. Her, she was standing alone, and then one time I came out of the hotel, and she was gone."

Devans picked up a pen. "You got a description?"

I shrugged. "For what it's worth. Too much make-up, hair the color of a cheap wig."

"Height and weight?"

"She wore heels, had stuffed herself into tight, flashy clothes. Those things distort."

Devans stopped writing. "That's not much help."

"If I could rattle off her stats the way they do on the cop shows, I'd be working that side of the desk."

He blanched, and I wondered whether I'd gone too far. Pointing a stubby finger at me he warned, "You don't want to get too smart for your own good."

Devans could keep me here for hours with his idiot questions. I didn't have hours, and the only way I saw to get back on the street was to involve myself further. I took the gamble. "Even if I don't have what you need, I could still help."

"And how do you figure to do that?"

"You tell me where she lives. I'll hang around. She'll panic and do something stupid. You pick up the pieces."

"Why do you want to know where she lives?"

Didn't I just answer that? "To make her nervous. Maybe she won't know me by sight, but she'll recognize the type."

Devans snorted. "And then what, you rob the place, we have her in lockup?"

I stiffened. "I would never do that."

"It always warms my heart to meet a whore with a conscience."

I savored several replies but managed to swallow them. I needed my freedom more than I needed to score points against this fat fuck. "If I can spook her, it could make your job much easier."

Devans tucked himself in. "We'll get her without you, but maybe you could help speed the process."

"Well, what are we waiting for?"

"We aren't waiting for anything. I'm trying to decide why I should trust you."

"Me? I want this solved as quickly and quietly as possible. Dead Johns are bad for business."

Devans stared at me with those blank eyes of his. "I don't want you shaking her down."

I shook my head. "The longer this goes on, the worse it is for me. I'm just trying to make a living, provide some sort of life for my little girl."

Devans made a raspberry sound, but I could tell I reached him. "The wife's name is Sharon. They live at 1212 Maple, but you can take your time hoofing it over there, since she'll probably be with the Captain for another hour. Now get out of here before I find some reason to detain you."

Leaving before Devans could change his mind, I knocked down three Johns, paid the rent with twenty minutes to spare, asked Wanda if she could babysit for a few hours longer.

Taking my least favorite wig from the bureau, I checked to make sure none of my hairs were stuck inside. Even if Devans forgot how I helped him panic the wife, the planted evidence would close the case for good.

I never would have killed the husband if he didn't start flashing the gun to impress me. I'd been sick as a dog for weeks, and there was no way I could earn what I needed in the time that was left. It was just his bad luck to think I wasn't desperate.

Sitting on the edge of the bed with him, I made my eyes go wide and asked him if I could touch it. The gun was heavier than I expected, but pulling the trigger was easier.

After stuffing the wig and one of my dresses into a plastic bag, I changed into jeans and a sweatshirt. No one would recognize me dressed like this.

I paused, tried to bring my beating heart under control. Today was a day of firsts. I'd never killed anyone before, and I'd never framed someone else for the crime.

Hey, if Sharon couldn't keep her husband out of the Atlantic, she wasn't worth crying over.

As I left the apartment and raced across town, my only nagging concern was whether Sharon had an alibi for the time of the killing. I figured I was mostly safe there, otherwise Devans wouldn't suspect her of doing the job herself. I just wished I knew for sure.

Maybe Sandra had no alibi because she'd actually been at the Atlantic. She could have been playing one of those suburban sex games with hubby, or better yet, checking up on him. She probably meant to kill him herself, and I'd done her a favor.

Maple wasn't so rich that there were gates and guards, but any one of these houses would cost more than I'd ever see. Their lawns probably cost more than I'd ever see.

The driveway was long, and by the time I reached the house, the bushes and trees hid the car from any neighbors. Grabbing my plastic bag, I realized with a start that of course the house would have a security system.

I did not need my day of firsts to include being arrested for breaking and entering after tripping a silent alarm.

Swearing, I tried to think of another plan.

Sharon was probably too smart to keep the wig and dress in the house where any maid could find them. Rushing back from the Atlantic, she wouldn't have had a lot of time to ditch the items, which left burying them in the trashcan before the police arrived with the news.

Leaving the safety of my car, I slipped through a gate to the back of the house. What did the rich do with their trash? I was sunk if it was locked up somewhere.

"Well, if it isn't the whore with a conscience."

I turned to see Devans gloating at me.

He held out a hand. "What do you have in the bag, something homemade for the grieving widow?"

I would have flung the bag at his fat face, but what was the point?

Sidework

He was one of those creatures who hunt through store catalogs for the perfect storage unit, foolishly believing it was necessary, even possible, to put a life in order, never mind keep it that way. My client in a nutshell.

So many of my clients in a nutshell.

I leaned back against the row of beer kegs, feeling the cold metal through my shirt. "You were right. Your wife is seeing somebody."

The muscles along his jaw tightened. "Do I know him?"

"I couldn't say. Didn't want to interrupt."

Jeremy kicked at the flooring. "Probably that coworker of hers."

"If you're interested, I can find out. I can also keep it from happening again."

He paled. "I don't believe in violence."

"That's not what I meant. I can put a scare into them, create the impression I'm coming at them from his end. Debra will be so relieved you never found out, she'll stay honest."

"Have you done this before?"

I nodded toward the building outside the walk-in refrigerator. "You manage a restaurant. Have you learned yet what keeps the place going, something they might not even have mentioned in that hospitality management program you aced?"

"What's that?" He puffed his chest, probably attempting to regain some shred of his manhood.

"Sidework. That's where your cooks, your bartenders, your servers spend two-thirds of their time. When it gets busy in the restaurant, you can't have your people prepping sauce and filling saltshakers. All those tasks are done at the beginning of their shift or at the end for the next."

Jeremy chewed that over. "Okay. Okay, just do it."

"We'll use a verbal contract for this portion, and I'll need the cash up front. That way, if anything goes wrong, you can't be implicated."

"What could go wrong?"

This from a guy who managed a restaurant, land of one crisis after another. "There's always a slight chance her boyfriend will try to mix it up with me. I might have to slug him a few times."

Jeremy's grin wasn't pretty. "Where do I not sign?"

The next day, I took photographs of Debra and her lover as they crossed from the office building to his car, and then another set as they ran from his car to the motel. Wouldn't it be ironic if the manager of that fine establishment graduated from the same school as my client?

Parked behind lover boy, I called an ex-client and waited for him to finish the traffic stop before running the tags. Then I drove to the address he gave me.

Timothy Ward lived in a brand-spanking-new development that went up twice as fast as its neighbors, thanks in no small part to words I'd whispered in some people's ears. I owed a gal a favor, and I always paid my debts. She made ten thousand when the last unit was completed a full seven months sooner than the earliest possible date claimed by the man she bet against.

Timothy's house boasted a two-car garage. Neither bay was filled with the oddball possessions that would collect if a car weren't parked there every night.

There was no sign of toys, bikes, or any other child-related minutia.

How unfortunate. Children always added weight to the prospect of blackmail.

"Can I help you?" A short-haired brunette watched me from her front step, one hand on the open door, ready to flee if she determined I was dangerous.

Walking to the edge of Timothy's driveway, I acted surprised. "Nobody seems to be home."

"Tim gets in about five-thirty. Eli a little past six. Are you a friend of theirs?"

"We were schoolmates." I threw out my arms with just a twinge of dramatic flair. "I guess our reunion is just going to have to wait. After all these years, what are another couple of hours?"

We smiled at each other, and I returned to my car so she could go back to whatever she'd been doing on the other side of that window when she'd spotted me.

Adjusting the plan to accommodate this new information, the following morning I went to work with Eli, two cars back and then in the same elevator. People deferred to him.

The fact that he had his own office was even more promising. His assistant said Mr. Graham had a few free minutes at ten o'clock. I said I'd wait and leafed through corporate propaganda until I was told he could see me now.

Eli Graham shook hands before motioning me to a seat. "You told my assistant we had some business."

"I'm a professional photographer in that I sell pictures that other people would pay to keep from being seen."

He measured me with his cool gaze. "It sounds like you're talking about blackmail."

"No, I'm a private eye. In the course of a current investigation, I took some pictures that might interest you."

"Let me guess. Tim with some skirt." Eli sniffed. "They don't mean anything to him. That's all you need to know."

So much for that idea. "I apologize for taking up your time."

"Good day."

My surveillance switched to Eli, and I shot dozens of pictures detailing his home-life and partner over the period of a week. I was finally rewarded for my patience when he escorted another friend to an AIDS clinic. The friend didn't look good.

While I would have preferred to make a little extra money off one of the players, I'd settle for fulfilling my obligations. Even after all the hours I had spent chasing down possible opportunities, I'll still come out ahead.

Calling Debra, I arranged to meet her that night while Jeremy worked at the restaurant.

Debra paused as she stepped inside the launderette.

"Mrs. Carpenter?"

"Yes?"

"We spoke on the phone." I smiled warmly. "There are seats in the back near the dryers."

"You said something about Timothy."

"Why don't we get comfortable first?" I led her to the

waiting area.

Debra sat across from me. "What do you want?"

"I'm hoping you can help me." I paused, took a deep breath. "I know you're having an affair. That's not what's important to me. I'm concerned about Tim."

"Tim?"

I nodded. "His partner, Eli, has been sleeping around. Perhaps he senses that you and Tim ... Anyway, one of Eli's lovers has been diagnosed with AIDS."

"Eli?" Debra blinked rapidly as she struggled to keep up.

"I can't tell Tim what's going on. He'd never believe me." I handed her an envelope containing selected pictures. "But you, Tim will believe you."

Debra glanced down at the envelope. "What is this?"

"Photographs. I don't know how you'll explain them to Tim, but you have to convince him to break off the relationship with Eli before he also becomes infected."

"And if it's too late?" The envelope trembled in her hands.

"We can only pray it's not." I stood. "Thank you. Thank you for everything."

Debra barely nodded as I left her there with her thoughts.

That night, at 2:32 a.m., to be exact, I received an enraged call from my client. "What did you do? I just got home, and Debra is gone! Cleared out!"

"Did she leave a note?" I rubbed my face with my free hand.

"Nothing! But her clothes are gone, and she's taken some items of sentimental value."

"At least it doesn't sound as if she's planning to jump

off a bridge. I'll be at your place first thing. Since you're probably not going to sleep anyway, keep looking for a note. Check all your voicemails, emails, everything."

"What did you do to me?"

"I'll bring coffees." Hanging up, I rolled over and immediately fell asleep, trusting my internal clock.

I woke at noon, jumped into a quick shower, and finally caught up with Jeremy at the restaurant.

"You said first thing!"

Not bothering to remind him I'd also promised coffee, I raised my hands in surrender. "You're not my only client."

He slammed his office door closed behind us. "You promised you'd take care of things!"

"So, did she leave a note?"

"Nothing. Why? Is finding farewell messages another service you offer?" Sitting behind his desk, he glared at me. "For an additional price?"

"If she didn't leave a note, she's expecting to come back. Debra doesn't want a piece of physical evidence to come between you, harming the reconciliation process." Jeremy had been slopping tomato sauce into a pan when I found him in the kitchen, and I couldn't take my eyes off the splatter pattern.

His eyes went wide. "I don't believe this. You'll say anything, won't you? I suppose Debra leaving me is actually part of your plan to keep her faithful."

"Where might your wife have gone?"

Jeremy leaned forward. "Why do you want to know? So you can bill me for checking up on her? Or maybe you're offering to pick her up because, just coincidentally, your car contains a taxi meter."

I kept my voice level, trying to defuse the situation.

"There's a good chance that she only wants a little time to think over what she's done. Once she realizes what she's missing, she'll be back."

"I don't want to hear any more of your self-serving theories." He stabbed his finger towards the door. "Just get out, and stay out. I don't want to ever see your face again."

I honored my client's request, assembling the rest of the story from assorted news items.

Debra must actually have given the envelope of photographs to Tim before she disappeared. While she was probably trying to be helpful, all she did was incite a screaming match between Tim and Eli that quickly escalated into violence.

The neighbor who called 911 was not identified, but I pictured the brunette who'd spoken to me as I fleshed out the events in my mind.

By the time the police arrived at the house, Tim had beaten Eli so badly that he slipped into a coma. Apparently, Eli and the man he'd escorted to the AIDS clinic were ex-lovers, a five-year-old relationship that still obviously threatened Tim for some reason.

The following day, that ex-lover shot Tim to death as Tim was being escorted to the courthouse. The police immediately subdued the killer, who did not resist arrest but laid down his weapon and raised his hands. As he later told reporters, there was no point in running since prison was as good a place to die as anywhere else.

After completing a thorough investigation and exhausting all possible leads, the police were unable to determine the origin of the photographs. Imagine that.

Jeremy didn't leave a note, so I can't say whether it was the loss of his wife or the attendant tragedies that pushed him over the edge. While he was usually the last to leave the restaurant on Friday nights, this past Friday he locked himself in the walk-in refrigerator and mixed three gallons of bleach with three gallons of ammonia.

While Jeremy's professors may have skipped the more mundane realities of the restaurant business, at least they'd covered the very serious dangers of accidentally producing chlorine gas while trying to clean and disinfect.

I tracked Debra to her folks' place in Maine. She'd suffered some kind of nervous breakdown, complicated by heavy drinking. Despite all the attention the story generated, nobody ever stepped forward, asking me to find the missing widow.

Just as accidents seem to unfold in slow motion, I watched in dismay as one possible revenue stream after another was lost to me.

Sure, Jeremy's check had cleared for the original infidelity investigation, and he paid cash for my follow-up work, but I still felt cheated. The whole situation had been so ripe with possibilities that it didn't seem fair I hadn't been able to tap additional resources.

And as if that wasn't bad enough, it didn't look like the case was going to generate any referrals either.

Smoking Gun

"Miss, can you tell us why you killed Maurice Sting?"

I felt like I should offer them something, but there were three cops in my kitchen, and I had just the one coffee cup. Still, it grated on my nerves, the waitress in me showing through, I guess.

"Miss?"

"There should be a law against bringing a child into this shithole of a world."

"Was Maurice Sting the father?"

"Dwight's father was a welcome pair of blue eyes on a gray day." I took a moment to recollect the rainy afternoon before continuing. "That Maurice Sting tormented my Dwight, made fun of him because he was slow. Maurice deserved what he got."

"Did he sexually abuse your son?"

"Get your mind out of the gutter." The question had come from the officer standing at the sink, smirky in his dark sunglasses. I turned back to the woman officer sitting at the table across from me. "Maurice tormented Dwight. When he heard my boy coming up the stairs, he would set rats loose on the landing. Dwight hates rats."

"So you shot Maurice Sting to stop him from doing that."

"I was protecting my son."

The other cop at the table flipped through his pad

again. "According to school records, Dwight was absent today."

"Would you feel like going to school, knowing rats were waiting for you when you came home?"

"Have you seen Dwight since you got out of work?"

"No." And I hoped he stayed away until the police were done questioning me. I was less concerned with being arrested than I was with Dwight getting involved. I even waived having an attorney present to speed this up.

Officer Sunglasses began pacing. "Do you always keep a loaded gun on the premises?"

"It was a gift."

"Someone gave you a gun?" Even his way of standing was belligerent.

I leaned forward, speaking to the female officer. "Dwight's father gave it to me. He said life was full of dangers, and he wanted me safe until he returned."

Officer Notepad shifted in his seat carefully, since that was the broken chair. "And has he ever returned?"

"Not yet." I honestly couldn't remember whether he promised to or whether I only imagined him saying the words. It didn't really matter either way. He was long gone.

Sniffing, Officer Sunglasses shook his head. "So what made you decide today of all days to shoot your neighbor?"

"It just kept piling up."

"What did?"

Sitting back, I crossed my arms. "Dwight was hysterical last night because of the rats."

"What about them?"

"Maurice Sting filled the stairwell with the nasty

creatures."

"You ever wonder if maybe it's just the building? I saw plenty of rats on my way up today, and Maurice Sting is dead in the morgue."

"My Dwight wouldn't lie."

The female officer smiled kindly as if she believed me. "Did you try to talk to Maurice about the problem, try to resolve things in a peaceful manner?"

"Some men, you just can't talk to."

Officer Sunglasses laughed. He was probably one of them.

Tapping his pen against the table, Officer Notepad asked, "What time would you say you went to Maurice's apartment?"

"I didn't happen to glance at the clock."

"Was it right after you came home? An hour later? Two? When did you shoot him?"

How did I answer? Were they trying to trip me up? When I came home and opened the closet to change, I noticed the shoebox had been moved. With a feeling of dread, I opened the lid. The gun smelled like the exhaust from a city bus.

I ran through the small apartment, calling for Dwight, but there was no sign of him. Trying to convince myself that he wouldn't have replaced the gun if he shot himself by accident, I calmed down enough to count the towels.

I found two bath, two hand, and one kitchen. Dwight wasn't hiding somewhere trying to stop the bleeding. My boy probably wasn't hurt.

Sitting at the kitchen table, I tried to think this out.

Dwight had carried on something fierce last night, sobbing about the rats, shaking in terror. It had taken me hours of soothing talk to pacify him.

Although Dwight was slow, he wasn't blind, deaf, and dumb. He knew about the neighborhood gangs, the corner drug dealers. There was no way to shield him from the violence of the streets when he couldn't help but notice it. Could my little boy have taken a cue from the punks and decided to stop his tormentor for once and for all?

Slipping the gun into the big pocket of my uniform, I prayed that I was wrong, that Maurice Sting would answer the door when I knocked.

When I knocked, the door swung open.

Officer Sunglasses brought me up short. "This being the first time you murdered someone, I'd expect the details to stick. It was your first time, wasn't it? Or maybe it wasn't. Maybe that's why Dwight's father hasn't been around."

I steeled myself. "When I came home from work and Dwight wasn't here, I decided to talk to Maurice Sting. I brought the gun because I thought putting a scare into him might help."

The female officer nodded to keep me talking. "And then what happened?"

"He invited me in and offered me a cup of coffee. He said it was the first time he offered a cup of coffee to a waitress. I told him why I was there, and he laughed in my face."

"So you shot him."

"He started making fun of Dwight. Then he came on to me, said we should get better acquainted. I couldn't make him stop, couldn't make him listen to what I was saying."

"And then?"

"I pulled the gun out of the pocket, pressed it against

his heart, and pulled the trigger."

I pushed his door open, and there he was, lying on the floor. *Oh, Dwight, what have you done, baby boy?* I walked toward the body in a daze. *Please let the red stain on his shirt be jelly. Let him sit up and yell at me for entering his apartment. Please God please.*

Maurice was dead.

I could have stood there wailing my anguish, but I knew I needed to act quickly if I was going to save my son. Maurice was already dead. Nothing was going to change that.

Grabbing his hair, I yanked him up to a sitting position and placed the barrel against the bullet wound in his chest. I closed my eyes and pulled the trigger.

Officer Notepad made a flapping sound as he flipped through his book. "A woman two apartments from Maurice thought she heard a gunshot around three o'clock. Does that sound right to you?"

How did that time relate to what I'd already said? Three o'clock. Dwight must have killed Maurice just minutes before I came home. It was a wonder we didn't pass on the stairwell.

"Maybe. I don't know."

"She wasn't sure either. It could have been yesterday."

Officer Sunglasses cleared his throat. "Who are you protecting?"

My blood went cold. "Protecting?"

"You come home from work, and the first thing you do is shoot your neighbor? We know you were there, because when you pulled the gun out of your pocket, you dropped one of your pens under the couch. Who else was there with you?"

"No one." Here I was on firm ground. Not even Maurice Sting had really been in the room with me, not anymore.

"All on your own, you just decided to go on a shooting spree."

"I told you how it was."

He grunted. "You single-handedly bested a man who had a long record of violent behavior. You expect us to believe that."

"I'm telling you I shot Maurice Sting. What more do you want?"

The female officer nearly cooed. "We just want to understand, to make sense of what happened here today."

"There is no sense to it. Like I said earlier, it's a shithole of a world." I sighed. "Who's going to take care of my boy now?"

Perhaps Dwight would be placed in a better neighborhood somewhere with people who could afford to take care of him right. They'd hire him tutors to help with his schooling. Maybe there was a scholarship for children of murderers.

Officer Sunglasses was pacing again. "So you shot Maurice Sting, and then you came back to your apartment to call the police."

I was being so careful with my answers that this question surprised me. "Where else would I call from?"

"The scene of the crime?"

"It didn't even cross my mind. And I wanted to check if Dwight was back from school yet. I don't know. I guess I wasn't thinking too straight."

"After all, you just killed someone."

"Yes. Yes, I did."

I heard the front door open and then Dwight's excited steps. He paused when he entered the kitchen, lowering his eyes against the police officers as he snuggled up next to me.

"Hi, Honey." I hugged him tight, praying the sense of security and love would stay with him.

He giggled into my ear. "Guess what, Mommy? I did it. I killed one of the rats. I shot him with your gun, and then I went and buried him in the park."

As the world began to spin, I held onto Dwight for dear life.

Tenant at Will

"I am so going to fuck you up."

Flipping my mother the bird, I continued going through her purse, desperate for a tampon. "Fuck is a verb, Janie. You'd actually have to drag yourself off that couch and do something."

"Everything I've done, I've done for you."

I tossed her purse back onto the table. "Name one thing."

"I gave you birth."

"Prematurely. And if you'd laid off the booze, you might have been able to carry me full term."

"You have always been an ungrateful bitch."

"Right. There's nothing worse than a newborn who keeps making demands. Didn't I understand you were sleeping it off? Why did I keep crying? Why did I insist on being fed?"

She grimaced. "Your father was smart to leave when he did."

"We'll never know, will we, since you didn't even get his name, never mind his thoughts on the matter."

"Ungrateful. Disrespectful. You're nothing but a disappointment to me."

"A disappointment? Who makes sure there's always a whiskey bottle next to you on the coffee table? Who buys the painkillers you keep stashed between the cushions?

Who cleans up your messes, the vomit and piss?"

"I'm your mother."

"No, you're a spoiled brat. Of course my father left. He was smart enough to recognize what you really were."

"You must be stupid, then, to stick around." Janie stuck out her tongue. "Maybe you're retarded."

I turned on my heel and stormed out of the room, continued out of the house, since I was already in motion, my panties telling me I might as well give up trying to find a tampon.

Stopping only when I could no longer hear my mother's cackling, I dropped onto a fallen log by the side of the road.

Today was just shitty. Plain and simple. First Carlos cancelled, and now this.

I needed to get out and have some fun. Low lights, loud music, and enough beer to blur the gaping vortex that was my mother. Carlos dancing close, whispering into my ear.

Instead, he had to meet with some people. "You'll see, Babe. I'm going to take you away from all this."

How many times had I heard that? Sure, the fact that Carlos was a business major on a full academic scholarship made him seem like my ticket out of here, but when? Just what is international finance anyway? Carlos said the career prospects were excellent, but of course they'd tell him that. They probably needed to keep the classes full.

Maybe I'd made a mistake betting on Carlos. I couldn't wait until he finished his degree. Until he landed that supposedly killer job. I wanted out now.

Carlos was all about promises, conservative like his police detective father. Carlos liked to discuss our future, make hypothetical plans, weigh the positive and negative aspects of honeymooning in Hawaii, or maybe Europe.

Bruce, he just wanted to bend me over the hood of his Camaro.

There was a certain appeal to that.

I could go to him this very minute, give him a whiff, and we'd be out of here as soon as he topped the tank, no questions asked. He'd been trying to get into my pants for years.

I jumped up and marched down the road to the complex where Bruce lived. It wasn't as if Carlos owned me. We saw each other. So what? Just because we'd talked marriage didn't mean I had to pretend other men didn't exist.

A tractor-trailer blew by, blasting me with a wall of hot air, its slipstream nearly sucking me into the path of an oncoming vehicle.

Bruce already had a real job. And wherever we went, there would always be restaurants looking to hire a dependable dishwasher. Bruce wasn't trapped by some fancy degree, shackled to the few places where he could find suitable work.

With Bruce, the sky was the limit. We wouldn't let anybody box us in. We'd answer to no one, free to go anywhere, any time we pleased.

I won't even go back to pick up my things. I'll buy everything new. Start fresh. I'll be reborn into a motherless world and grab life with both hands.

Bruce can make that happen. Not Carlos. All Carlos could do was trace my cheekbones with gentle fingertips as he spun his fairytale fantasies. The man was a dreamer.

As I reached Bruce's complex, I caught him pulling out

of the driveway, the Camaro spotless. I waved until he stopped.

Bruce lowered his window. "You looking for me?"

"You bet." I bent down to lean on the doorframe. "Where are you off to in such a hurry?"

"Family Buffet. I'm running late."

"Mind if a tag along?" Bending lower than necessary, I let gravity work to my advantage.

"Why?"

"I was thinking maybe a little detour ... "

Bruce blinked as if he didn't catch my drift. "I really have to get to the restaurant."

"Forget it." Men. I turned and started walking, not even waiting for him to drive away first. Work wasn't going anywhere. I was.

Kicking a rock out of my way, I realized I should have known better than to trust someone whose lease was tenant-at-will. How dependable was that?

Of course, now I was back where I started, stuck with two choices and no alternatives. Make that one choice, since no way was I continuing with this shit.

As I walked home, I rejected one plan after another until I found the perfect scenario. How could I not have thought of it sooner? I'll tell you how. I'd been waiting for Bruce and Carlos.

Well, not any more. Once the police said they were satisfied my mother's death was an accident, I was history. After the funeral was over, anyway. Since the cops would wonder if I skipped town before pretending to grieve, I was actually going to have to bury Janie.

What was the point?

It wasn't as if there were any friends or family who

wanted to mourn her, who needed a gravesite so they could pay their respects.

Science. I could donate her body to science. Let them figure out why it was so well preserved. Damn. Maybe the donation would be a tax write-off.

As soon as I entered the house, I could hear my mother snoring. Dead to the world. Sweet.

Somewhere under that rippling bag of flesh was her stash of pills. Everybody knew that painkillers and alcohol were a deadly combination. Maybe even Janie knew the dangers involved. Suicide worked, too.

After carefully moving the coffee table out of the way, I knelt next to her and forced my hands under the cushions. Pinned by her weight, I could just barely move my fingers, but at least Janie was too lazy to do anything but keep the plastic bag close to the edge.

Nothing.

I stood and leaned over her to run my hands along the back of the cushions, Janie's breath almost enough to make me gag.

Gotcha.

I placed a handful of pills in the half-empty class of whiskey on the coffee table and then topped it off.

The pills just sat there.

"Dissolve!"

Janie shifted.

As soon as she settled back down, I ran to the kitchen for a spoon. If stirring didn't do it, I didn't know what to try next. Maybe warming the booze, but then I'd have to cool it again.

Nothing was ever easy.

The pills finally began to disappear into the brown

liquid.

That step completed, I pushed at Janie's flab. "Wake up."

"Wah?"

"Wake up." I pushed her again, almost hard enough to rock the couch. "Did anybody call for me?"

"What do you want?" Janie grabbed the glass of whiskey from my hand and drained half of it.

"Did the phone ring while I was gone?"

Wiping the back of her arm against her mouth, Janie mumbled, "Check the machine."

"I thought Carlos might have called."

"How the fuck should I know?" My mother shook her head in disgust before finishing the whiskey. She handed me the glass before closing her eyes again.

"Thanks for everything, Mom."

I sat in the chair at the other side of the room and listened to her snore, wondering how long this was going to take. It didn't really matter, I guess. Neither of us was going anywhere.

Afterward, I'd have to wipe the bottle, glass, and plastic bag. Make sure hers were the only prints. Clean the spoon and return it to the drawer. What else did I have to do before calling 911? Change my underwear for one thing.

Her chest suddenly convulsed.

Vomit bubbled from her mouth, filling the room with its familiar stench. As Janie started to roll, I rushed to her side. Forced her head upright with one hand, her jaw closed with the other.

Her eyes sprang open as she started to flail.

I looked away and held on until she stopped moving.

The doorbell rang.

I froze. Wait. There was nothing to worry about. Probably just Bruce. He'd punched in late once too often, and they'd finally shit-canned his ass.

Bruce, I could deal with.

After stripping off my vomit-covered shirt, I tossed it aside and went to open the front door. Just tell Bruce to wait in the car until I threw on some clothes. And then later, let him discover the body.

No, that wasn't going to work. I hadn't been able to deal with the fingerprints yet.

Carlos grinned at me. "Surprise."

"I thought you had to meet with some people." I placed my hand on the door jam, blocking the entrance.

"We're done." Carlos looked past me. "Can I come in?"

"How about I meet you outside once I'm dressed?"

His eyes widened. "What's that behind you?"

As I turned to look, Carlos slipped under my arm and inside the house. "I can't believe you fell for that."

"Kindergarten was a long time ago." I leaned back against the open door, folding my arms behind my back. "Why don't we go for a drive?"

"With you dressed like that?" Carlos walked deeper into the house before turning to face me again. "I don't remember you answering the door half-naked before, not that I'm complaining."

"You blew me off." I needed to get Carlos out of here as quickly as possible. I didn't know how much they could narrow the time of death, but Carlos was no dummy. "In fact, I was thinking about going to bed early. Since you were too busy for me anyway."

"No, Babe, I was making plans. I told you that." He

nearly bounced from one foot to the other. "First I met with a jeweler, who sold me this."

"What?" I squinted to see what he was holding, but the light was wrong.

"Here."

I caught what he tossed, one of those velvet boxes, the kind that contain a ring. "Wah?"

"Then I met with the guy who owns that apartment complex up the street. You'll still be close to your mother. Stop in any time you want." Carlos flashed a smile almost wide enough to decapitate him. "We can move in tomorrow."

"Carlos ..."

"I'm serious. Once he heard who my father was, he said he wouldn't even bother running a check on me." He motioned me closer. "Come on. Let's tell your mother the exciting news."

Carlos padded down the hall before I could get a word in edgewise. And what would I say, even if I could stop him? That my mother had stepped out for a minute?

I watched Carlos disappear into the living room. Imagined him catching sight of her. The table out of place. The bag of pills and the spoon. My shirt.

Carlos would put it all together before he even finished pulling out his phone to call his precious daddy.

Janie managed to fuck me up after all.

And she didn't need to move off the couch to do it.

Unweaving the Rainbow

The only guy in the packed bar, Joey took one long look and then snorted in derision. "Bunch of bull dykes."

"You know, some of the people present might be offended by your use of that term." Including the woman at the next table who could hurl his scrawny ass through the front window without putting down her cabernet.

"Why? Is it my fault they don't like dick?"

"That's quite possible." I paused. "You have some information for me."

"Maybe I do."

Oh, he was a sly one. "Listen, Joey. You dragged me all the way out here because you knew I'd pay for the privilege of hearing how smart you are."

His thin lips attempted to swallow each other. "I don't think I like your attitude. This place rubbing off on you?"

"Cut the crap." There went my bid for Most Courteous Private Investigator. "I haven't slept in two days. You have something to say, say it. Otherwise, I'm history."

"You got the money?"

"Tell me what you know, and it's yours."

He crossed his arms in a feeble attempt to intimidate me. After spending three hours wallowing in the idea of the two hundred dollars I'd offered for information, no way was he going to settle for a free draft beer.

Joey sniffed. "I was making a delivery. You know?

And, ah, I was wondering what I'd done for Dana Cooke lately. That's when I saw the old lady."

"Any old lady in particular?"

"The one I hear you're looking for. Miss Keats."

"Mrs. Sweeney?" My client's mother.

He shrugged. "She was Miss Keats when she taught third grade."

Having Joey on her résumé had probably been reason enough to change her name. "And where did you see her?"

"Leaving that little playground on Bradford. Had a kid with her."

"Recognized her from the flyers?" I'd emphasized Sweeney wandered away from Nickerson Assisted Living, letting people assume Alzheimer's rather than the truth.

"She was just how I remembered her. Staring up at that mug all day." Joey cleared his throat. "Speaking of another mug ... "

"Don't leave with anybody else while I'm gone." Rather than wait for the server make her next appearance, I went up to the bar and ordered a draft.

The bartender deadpanned, "Your girlfriend sure is ugly."

"You should see her naked." I winked as I pushed my change back across the mahogany.

Joey was staring down a party of four.

"Here's your beer."

"Hm." He drained half. "Where was I?"

"Hanging around a playground."

He stiffened. "I was driving by. Lucky for you."

Maybe if I played lightning rod, I could keep him from antagonizing the clientele. "That's all you have? You saw someone who reminded you of your third-grade teacher?"

"You wish. Soon as I recognized Miss Keats, I went around the block and parked. Watched where she went."

"And that would be?"

"Let's see that money."

I took ten twenties from my bag and handed him five. "Go on."

Joey licked his lips as if hide his smile. "She entered the inn next door. While I was waiting for you to arrive, I kept an eye on the front door in case she left."

"That why you asked to meet here?"

He nodded. Lowered his voice. "Also didn't want anybody seeing me talk to you."

Apparently, the people around us didn't count. Or maybe Joey was just worried about his kind of people, bottom-feeders who would never be caught dead in a place like this, alcohol being the devil's brew.

"You get the second hundred when I confirm she's there."

"But she could have left while we were inside!"

"Next time, talk faster." I stood. "Can I assume I'll find you in your car?"

"Make sure you do."

I left him with the last word to restore whatever manhood he might have felt he lost sitting in this bar and walked through a warm drizzle to the Victorian bed and breakfast.

A woman wearing a button-down shirt straightened from the dinner table she'd been setting. "Can I help you?"

"I'm here about one of your guests, a Mrs. Sweeney."

"Yes?"

"Do you know if she's in her room?"

The woman smiled. "One always knows when a child

is present in an older house." Her statement was punctuated by sound of pounding feet.

"I think I'll be able to find them on my own."

The stairs creaked under the carpeting, and ocean scenes climbed through the seasons until I reached summer at the landing.

Laughter came through the closed door on my left. My knock stopped it.

Mrs. Sweeney blinked. "Are we being too loud?"

"Not as far as I'm concerned." I waved to the four-year-old girl hugging her grandmother's leg. "You must be Abigail."

She nodded. "Are you a friend of Gram's?"

"I hope to be."

With a downcast sigh, Mrs. Sweeney opened the door and shuffled aside to let me in. "Would you care for a seat?"

"Thanks." I chose the chair I thought she'd have difficulty escaping. "How's your vacation?"

She winced at my word-choice. "Lovely, although a light rain has been in the forecast."

"It was drizzling when I came up the walk." I examined the room, decorated by hand with items crafted by people. "Beautiful place for a little getaway."

"Yes. Before the children were born, my husband and I came here every year. This is the very room where we spent our honeymoon." She paused. "Abigail, why don't you draw a picture for our guest?"

The girl leapt to get her art supplies and then plunked down in the middle of the hardwood floor.

I kept my eyes on Abigail. "With the weather, you probably want to cut your trip short."

"Did my daughter send you?"

I nodded. "They didn't want to involve the authorities."

"I'm sure they don't. Imagine the boardroom whisperings. That house is not a suitable home."

"I've been there." I faced Mrs. Sweeney. "This is not a viable solution, however. If I may be so bold, I'd suggest hiring a lawyer to help you navigate the legal system."

Mrs. Sweeney wrapped her hands together. "We have plans for the morning. Abigail wishes to visit the waterfront so that she can collect some shells."

The tiny body tensed, interrupting the flow of her crayon arcs.

"That sounds delightful. Unfortunately, I need to return to Standish today."

Abigail looked up.

"Finish your drawing. I'm sure you'll see me sometime at home. It was a pleasure meeting you."

Mrs. Sweeney walked me to the door. "They can afford a much better class of lawyer."

"I know one who specializes in custody cases. I'll call you at Nickerson once my current business is resolved."

The sun was peeking through clouds thinned by a sea breeze. Joey rolled down his window as I approached.

"Well?"

I handed him the second hundred. "Thanks for the heads up."

Joey fanned the twenties. "Looks like my son'll be getting those sneakers after all."

"Do yourself a favor. Once he has them, take him somewhere and play ball."

Joey gave me a strange look. "Sure."

I patted the roof of his car before returning to my own.

Whacking for Gomez

I must have been strangling this asshole for twenty minutes when somebody shot him dead.

Pushing the body away from me in disgust, I wiped my face to see his blood on my hands. Damn. That's why I never used a gun. It was just too messy.

Scott stepped into the room, keeping his gun aimed at the dead man as he approached the body to give it a kick.

"You crazy fuck, you could have killed me."

He grinned. "Not unless the bullet took a left turn after leaving his heart."

"I'll give you a left turn. What's the idea shooting someone I'm in the middle of killing?"

"Gomez paid me to whack him."

I was stunned. "But Gomez paid me to whack him."

Scott shrugged. "Sorry, but I think I'm the official cause of death."

"I was killing him long before you arrived. Don't you have any sense of ethics?"

"It's like the hairy tortoise story. He who crosses the finish line first, wins." Scott stuck the gun in his pocket but I noticed his hand didn't stray far.

"If I wasn't holding him still, you never would have made the shot."

"Still?" Scott laughed. "Except for his neck, he was dancing all over the place."

"Yeah, I think that neck had cement holding the steel rods in place. I've never known anyone so hard to strangle. My thumbs are nearly broken." They weren't that bad, but I wanted Scott to think I was less dangerous than I was. They didn't call me The Grip for nothing.

"He shot real easy."

"Only because I was keeping him busy."

Scott nodded, screwed up his eyes as though he was thinking. "Look, no hard feelings. I mean I'm the one who shot him, but maybe I can cut you in. I'll tell Gomez you were like my assistant or something."

He was lucky he was carrying that gun. The only way I'd be his assistant is if I could assist him six feet under. "What kind of cut are you proposing?"

"Ninety-ten."

"Fifty-fifty. I was here first."

"Eighty-twenty."

"Sixty-forty. Plus, you're getting the credit."

"Seventy-thirty."

I flexed my fingers. After the dead guy, Scott would be an easy strangle. The only problem was I was far enough away that he'd have no trouble digging that gun out of his pocket. "Fifty-fifty, but you ask Gomez for more money, so there's enough to split with no one feeling pinched."

Scott laughed. "You ask Gomez for more money, you want it so badly. I'll take my grand and disappear into the sunset, thank you very much."

"A grand?"

"Yeah, a grand." He examined his fingernails. "Cash on delivery."

I hooted. When I saw it made him mad, I hooted again. "Gomez promised me three."

"Three what?"

"Three grand."

Scott turned a deeper shade of red. "He was going to pay you three grand, and he only offered me one? That cheap prick."

"Everybody knows you have to pay for quality." I tried not to gloat, remembering the gun in his pocket.

"Quality?" He snorted. "The way it looked from the doorway, you were engaged to the guy."

I didn't like the sound of that. "Speaking of the stiff in question, the job isn't quite done yet. Your kill, your disposal problem."

"That's the kind of detail I leave to my assistant." He gave me a smile that bordered on glee.

I shook my head. "I'm not the one who shot him all up. You like blood, you put him in your car."

"Kick back three hundred of your cut."

I moved closer. "Before I did that, I'd steal a hearse and transport him myself."

"If we're going to share the profits, we should share the cleaning expenses. Two hundred."

"You're crazy. I'd torch this place first. Then if they find anything at all in the rubble, it will be your bullet."

Scott's hand kept brushing his pocket. "You know, maybe I should just tell Gomez that the guy killed you before I had a chance to shoot him. That way, maybe Gomez will give me the three grand and maybe even a bonus."

I wanted to stop this kind of thinking cold. "Like you said, Gomez is a cheap prick. He'd never give you more than he offered to pay you. Splitting with me is your best bet."

Scott nodded reluctantly. "So what are we going to do about the stiff?"

"I was planning to dump him in the soup. There are so many bodies dropped into that swamp, I think the water level rises two inches every year." I paused. "Of course, that only worked before you filled him full of holes."

"I only shot him once. One shot, one kill. And what, he can't go into the swamp if he was shot?"

"They find a body with a bullet hole, he didn't fall overboard while fishing."

"Who the fuck goes fishing in the swamp?"

"Considering the number of guys who have fallen overboard, at least a dozen by my count alone." I took another few steps closer to my target.

Scott sniffed. "Frankly, I don't think one bullet hole is going to make all that much of a difference. Who knows? Maybe it was a hunting accident. It could happen. He was trying to shoot fish in a barrel of toxic waste."

"Not in my car, and I'm not kicking back a dime."

Scott rolled his eyes. "If you're so worried about blood stains, we can transport him in my trunk."

"We? You suggesting we both go out there?"

His grin was skeletal, which made me wonder if he planned on returning alone. "Sure. That way we can both be certain that the other isn't going to Gomez on the sly."

"I hear what you're saying." Scott was still out of reach, but as long as he kept talking, I'd keep moving closer. "It would be awkward if we each went to Gomez separately claiming the kill and asking for payment."

"Cheap prick probably wouldn't pay either of us."

"You could always shoot him a few times as a convincer."

"Or you could massage the tickle out of his throat."

My fists automatically clenched. Maybe Scott was trying to piss me off so he could shoot me in self-defense. If so, it wasn't a very good idea. At the very least, he needed to learn some respect, and I knew just the way to teach him.

I was just about to take another step closer when I heard a gasp from the doorway, like someone startled a duck.

We both spun, but the guy was gone before we could move. I started to take off after him, but with his lead, I was never going to catch up. Besides, I wasn't so comfortable putting Scott in a position where he could shoot me in the back.

Hitmen didn't exactly subscribe to the buddy system.

I turned to find Scott leaning over the body, flipping through a wallet. What a fucking vulture.

While Scott's neck was exposed and he didn't have eyes in the back of his head, I'd need some kind of garrote to strangle him from this angle, and I forgot to bring one. This was supposed to be a simple hit. I'd have to wait for another opportunity. "We'd better get a move on before he calls the cops."

Scott swore a blue streak. "I've got some bad news. You were strangling the wrong person."

"What are you talking about?"

He stood. "According to the cards in his wallet, this stiff is someone named John Siam." He tossed the wallet onto the body. "I bet that was our bird in the doorway."

"You shot the wrong guy?"

Scott licked his lips. "This was the right address, and he fit the description."

I almost giggled. "You shot the wrong fucking guy."

"Hey, who are you to mouth off?" He turned belligerent again. "You were strangling him when I got here."

"Yeah, but I didn't kill him."

"You were doing your damnedest."

"Maybe I was just massaging the tickle out of his throat." I changed the subject before Scott could top my reply. "You ever heard of this John Siam?"

"Shit, no. The name doesn't mean anything to me. I just hope he wasn't a good friend of Gomez."

Now that would be bad news. "Maybe Gomez hired him, too. I wonder how much more he was offered than you were."

Scott ignored my comment and motioned toward the doorway. "So what do we do now? Our bird has flown, and we aren't going to be able to surprise him a second time."

"Hell, for all we know, that guy was another hired gun."

"Squawking like that?"

I shrugged. "So he was expecting a hit, not a convention."

Scott kicked the dead man another couple of times. "You were the first to mis-identify the guy. What are you going to tell Gomez?"

"I'm thinking I might say I was asking him questions when you busted in and shot him to death. Now I got a dead stiff and no leads on the guy Gomez wants whacked."

At that, Scott pulled the gun from his pocket and started waving it around. "You might want to rethink your story. Or I might have to tell Gomez that when I came into the room, I heard the two of you planning to sell Gomez down the river, so I shot the both of you."

"He wouldn't believe it for a minute."

"There will be no one left alive to contradict me. I think that reopens the negotiations at ninety-ten."

"Fifty-fifty." I inched forward.

"Eighty-twenty, and you get to live."

"Fifty-fifty, and you don't have to sleep with a gun under your pillow."

"Ninety-ten. I always have and always will."

"Hey, you went the wrong way. You're supposed to go lower, not higher."

"You can't shoot a guy for trying, especially when he's the one with the gun." He waggled it to emphasize his edge.

I shook my head. "Look, the cops are going to come charging through the door any minute now. The hell with the body. Let's just leave and worry about who gets what later."

Scott stuck the gun back in his pocket. "For once, the man is right. We won't have anything if we end up in jail."

Staying out of each other's reach, we slipped out and made our way down to street level to find a commotion outside. Our bird, the guy from the doorway, was lying in the middle of the road, banged all to hell.

There were a half-dozen cops taking statements, a few photographers hunting for gore that the others had missed. Lights were flashing, and police tape was going up like tinsel. It was a celebration that the guest of honor would probably have just as soon skipped.

Scott and I both said we didn't see nothing, didn't hear

nothing. It was strange not lying to a cop. Part of me wanted to make something up so I wouldn't sound like such a dud.

Glancing up the street, I noticed Gomez sitting behind the wheel of a Buick, one of those colors that defy description. When he saw me looking at him, he flipped me the finger and pulled off into traffic.

That son of a bitch.

I turned, caught Scott's eye, and we both shrugged in unison. *Fuck it.* I started to walk away, knowing that Scott wasn't about to shoot me in the back with all these witnesses, and what was the point? There was nothing to split, and it no longer mattered whether we wanted ninety-ten or fifty-fifty.

Gomez had used us to flush the guy out and then did the job himself. Scott was right. That Gomez was some cheap prick.

Where's the Beef

Mac lowered his voice as he topped off my coffee. "If you're looking for work, the guy at the end of the counter could use your help."

Leaning back, I assessed Mac's recommendation: late twenties, clean-shaven, shoulders of a former college linebacker. Probably a middle manager wondering why his wife wasn't as frisky as she used to be. He huddled over his cup. If this were a bar, he'd be well on his way to becoming a sloppy drunk. Instead, his hands would shake all afternoon.

He didn't seem in a hurry. I finished my breakfast, careful not to get any on me, and walked over to see what he needed. Up close he was even more All-American, only the disheartened slouch keeping him from being a poster boy for milk.

Nodding towards an empty booth, I said Mac had sent me.

"Who's Mac?"

"The guy behind the counter. He told me you could use a PI."

Linebacker came off the stool so quickly he knocked his spoon clattering to the floor. "Do I ever."

By the time I picked up after him, he was seated with his hands folded on the table. Signaling Mac with two raised fingers I joined my new best friend. "So what seems to be the problem?"

He held out his hand. "Tim Alison, Assistant Manager, Berkshire Steakhouse, pleased to meet you. We've experienced some slippages, and they've been traced to my shifts."

"Are you responsible?"

Tim puffed up. "I wouldn't be Assistant Manager if I wasn't."

"I meant whether you were responsible for the slippages."

He couldn't have looked more surprised if I punched him. "Of course I didn't steal anything. The problem is, I don't know who did."

Mac arrived with the two coffees. When he stood right next to me, the stains on his apron left little to the imagination. "Get you guys anything else?"

Tim shook his head.

"We're fine, thanks." I watched Tim spoon in sugar as if the caffeine wasn't doing enough for him.

"So you're really a private investigator?"

"You'll know for sure when you get my bill. What kind of slippages?"

Tim slurped and then smacked his lips. "Hamburger."

"Hamburger."

He nodded. "Everything's computerized at Berkshire Steakhouse. A Texas Max is eight ounces of hamburger, a Double Beef is six, and a bowl of chili is four. At the end of the shift I run a report that might say I sold a hundred of each item. That adds up to a certain amount of hamburger accounted for."

"Eighteen hundred ounces."

Tim sat back dumbfounded. "How'd you do that?"

"I was naive enough to pay attention in school. Go on."

Shaking his head in amazement, Tim continued. "Of course, people make mistakes, and then we fill out an Inventory Exception Form. Those get added into the calculations. You know, last week's ending inventory plus deliveries minus sales plus IEFs minus this week's inventory should equal zero."

"What kind of controls are in place? A hundred Double Beefs averaging six and a quarter ounces would throw off your reckoning by more than four burgers."

Tim's jaw dropped. "Why aren't you teaching at a college or something?"

"I slugged the Dean of Academic Affairs. She didn't much appreciate it."

"You hit a woman?"

"She was drunk at the time. How do you know the Double Beef is only six ounces?"

He was slow to catch up. "Oh, digital scales. We weigh everything. And even if the prep cook didn't pay attention, the readings are captured in the computer. I've seen the reports, and they're clean."

"How much missing hamburger are we talking here?"

"A pound a shift."

I'd never investigated a misdemeanor before. "For what you're going to pay me, you could replace two years' worth of missing hamburger and then some."

He winced. "I don't have two years. The Regional Supervisor wants this problem solved before more people decide they can get away with it. My job is on the line."

My last case, I'd tumbled down a stairwell while trading punches with a guy who didn't want to appear in court. The previous case, I was jabbed with a letter opener.

"How do you want me to proceed?"

If Puppy-Dog Boy wasn't sitting on his tail, it would have been wagging. "I can take you to the restaurant now, give you a feeling for the place before anyone comes in. Then I guess you just catch the thief."

All investigations should be this easy. "You said the slippages were traced to your shift. Who else works those particular hours?"

"Berkshire Steakhouse utilizes the team approach. I always work with the same group of people. I hire them. I train them. If need be, I fire them. They're my people."

"Any of them bear a grudge?"

"Against me? I'm the team leader. They're my people."

Clients, you had to love them. After explaining my rates to the Moses of fast food and paying for the coffee as my first reasonable expense, I let Tim lead me across town to the scene of the crime.

He wasn't a bad driver, if you didn't count the missed stop signs. At least he didn't get the sudden bright idea of playing lose-the-detective.

When we reached the restaurant, I discovered Berkshire Steakhouse had become a *bona fide* crime scene. There were half a dozen cruisers with lights flashing and a smear of yellow tape blocking the entrance to the parking lot.

Tim grabbed the first empty spot on the street and was already arguing with the police by the time I caught up to him.

"But I'm the Assistant Manager."

"I'm sorry, Sir. No one goes in."

Tapping Tim on the shoulder, I told him I'd handle this.

As my client stormed off, Officer Mendes shook his head. "Is he with you?"

"More like I'm with him."

"You got yourself a real hothead this time."

I nodded towards the restaurant. "And what do you have?"

"Kid skateboarding found a body out back, called it in on his cell phone."

"Ain't technology grand. Some jogger cutting through the lot suffer a heart attack?"

"Of sorts. He was shot twice in the chest."

"Any ID?"

Mendes smiled. "I'm not doing your job for you, am I?"

"I'll put a word in for you with the Chief."

"The Chief hates your guts."

"I'll make it a bad word." Tim paced the perimeter as if checking for a weakness.

Mendes turned to scream at a car that must have been going twice the speed limit. "Don't those assholes know how to rubberneck?"

"So what do you have on the victim?"

"He's a minor, so I can't release the name. What I can tell you is he had a Berkshire Steakhouse paycheck in his wallet." Mendes stepped closer. "And get this. Guess what we found when we pried open his fingers."

"A cryptic clue to the killer's identity?"

"Ball of raw hamburger. I guess someone had a beef with him." Mendes cracked himself up.

I grinned to be friendly. "Any leads?"

"Don't you get it? Had a beef with him."

"Very funny. Keep helping me, and maybe I'll put you in touch with a comedy writer."

"Think he'd have some fresh material for me?" Mendes nudged me with his elbow. "Fresh?"

"I'll pay the bill myself."

Mendes swore. "Man, no wonder the Chief hates you. I bet you don't appreciate his jokes, either."

"No, but I laugh whenever he holds a press conference." I glanced over at Tim, making sure he hadn't decided to rush the tape. "Tell you what. I understand the need to protect the identity of a minor. That's why I'm not asking you to give me his first name, just a word that rhymes with it. If you can see your way to helping me out, I'll send you ten pounds of something which rhymes with break."

Mendes licked his lips. "Crank."

"Thanks. I have to admit you fooled me. I never would have tagged you as someone who liked fruitcake."

I was three steps away before he thought of a reply. "I'll arrest you for being an asshole without a permit."

Hearing Mendes shout at me, Tim finally snapped, and I had to dig in with both heels to keep him from spending the rest of the day in jail. Then it took all my strength to push him back towards the cars. "Down, tiger."

"You don't have to take that kind of abuse from him. He's a public servant."

"I wouldn't say that too loudly."

Tim huffed and puffed. "I'm a taxpayer."

"Is there a Frank on this team of yours?"

My client was talking to me, but his eyes were on Mendes. "Yeah, Frank is one of my busboys. Frank Clements. What about him?"

"I think he's dead in the parking lot."

Tim froze, but I could see his mind crawling all over

the news, trying to make sense of it. "What do you mean, dead? Frank is just a kid. He worked last night. He's never skipped a shift like some of the others. He was never any trouble."

"He's got two bullets in him. He also has a handful of hamburger."

"I don't understand."

"That's what you're paying me for. You head on home, and I'll call you when I have something concrete."

Back in my car, I got in touch with my brother, the resident gossip and know-it-all. "How goes the soul-saving business?"

"Excellent, except for the fact I haven't managed to sign you up as a client."

"They say selling starts when the customer says no."

"God prefers a more subtle approach."

I'd never have guessed that from the way my brother acted. "While we're on the subject of subtle, you hear anything interesting about hamburger?"

"I hear it grills well. Maybe you can come over Saturday afternoon, and we can test the theory."

"I'm buried with paperwork. Anything else?"

"Just the terrible situation over at the Hindu temple."

"What situation?"

My brother sighed. "You don't even follow local news?"

"I hate to see my clients repeating their mistakes."

"In that case, I'll summarize. Someone has been flinging raw hamburger at the temple. You can imagine the reaction."

"Nasty. Any suspects?"

"We were discussing this at the interfaith meeting yesterday."

My brother was not one to be rushed through a story, which was fine so long as he didn't start quoting scripture to me. "And what were people saying?"

"There is a young lady of tender age who has been forbidden by her parents to see an older boy. Though age and not religion was the reason for concern, the timing suggests that the hate crime may be linked. Proverbs 14:30 says a tranquil mind gives life to the flesh, but passion makes the bones rot."

"Do you have a name for the boy?" Does it rhyme with crank?

"Nathan. He is not a member of my church or any other that we were able to determine."

Frank stole hamburger for Nathan, and an argument turned fatal. Frank tried to stop Nathan from stealing the meat and died for his efforts. Neither scenario made sense. Who would kill over a pound of hamburger? "I don't suppose you have a last name."

"I was not the one selected to speak to Nathan. If I remember correctly, however, he works at the supermarket on Westerly. That's where he and the young lady met."

"Thanks." Disconnecting, I pulled out into traffic.

If Nathan worked at a supermarket, he could damn well steal his own hamburger. Maybe a syndicate was at work. Maybe while Frank stole the hamburger, Nathan was in charge of obtaining buns. I should see if anyone was missing a bag of onions.

Inside the supermarket, I was directed to the canned food aisle, where I found Nathan standing in front of a soup display, hands on his hips.

"Nathan?"

He turned. "Can I help you?"

I handed him a twenty. "I borrowed this from Frank last night. He said I should give it to you, since I wouldn't see him before I leave for my trip."

"Sure. I'll give it to him tonight." Nathan raised his hand to stifle a yawn. "Sorry."

"Up late?"

He glanced down for a second before rolling his eyes. "It's embarrassing."

Silence and a welcoming face were a PI's best friends.

Nathan shrugged. "I spent the night outside my girlfriend's house, rushed home this morning to take a shower before coming here."

"Fight?"

"I wish. Her parents have forbidden her to see me. They say she's too young. Can you believe forbidding a relationship in this day and age?"

"Your parents are different?"

"It's just me and Frank." Nathan began to pace in circles. "But I'm crazy about Sachi, and not being able to see her is tearing me apart. I'm even spilling my guts to you, and you're a complete stranger." Nathan shook his head. "Love can be a killer. You know what I mean?"

"I do."

The store's PA system crackled to life. "Nathan C., please report to the front office. Nathan C. to the front office."

"Duty calls. Don't worry, I'll give Frank the money. And hey, thanks for listening."

"No problem."

I hadn't beaten the police by much, but it was enough. Nathan hadn't known his brother was dead. He also probably wasn't involved in the hamburger scheme, or he'd question why there wasn't any when he arrived home this morning.

Back in my car, I called Mister Holier-than-thou.

"I was wondering if you could talk to your counterpart at the temple. I'm looking for a name."

"Are you expecting me to rough him up if he doesn't talk?"

"Try not to let the discussion escalate into a brawl. I need to know the most likely candidate to respond to the hamburger-slinging with violence."

"If I help you solve your case sooner, you'll get a jump on that paperwork that keeps you from breaking bread with your brother."

I almost laughed. Which Biblical verse advocated blackmail? "Yes, I could probably join you on Saturday."

"There is an angry young man who goes by the name Indra, in Hindu mythology the God of War and Rain, Lord of Wind. I'll see you Saturday at noon."

After getting enough details to track Indra down, I tipped an imaginary hat to my brother. "If I'm late, make mine medium rare."

Since Indra was yet another young man, I made my usual rounds of the convenience stores and gas stations. I hit the music store, the burger joints. Two kids who admitted knowing Indra hadn't seen him for a few days.

The police could blanket-search better, but I owed my client more than simply tipping the law. Besides, I still had nothing more than conjecture.

A young lady outside a launderette suggested I try the public library.

Nathan is heartbroken. His kid brother blames

religious intolerance and responds in kind. Indra sees the hate crime and raises the stakes to murder. The story was tragic enough, and the motive stupid enough, to make me think it was probably true.

I wondered how my client would react when all he'd wanted was for the numbers to line up correctly.

At the library, I started in the reference room. Indra had signed up to use Internet Station 5, and that's where I found him.

"I'd like you to come to the police station with me."

Indra stuck out his lower lip and crossed his arms, the very picture of petulant defiance. "And why should I?"

"Because if you turn yourself in, you just might not spend the rest of your life behind bars."

The lower lip trembled. "I don't know what you're talking about."

I glanced at the computer monitor, saw a picture of his namesake killing a dragon. "If you want, I'll suggest a lawyer. If you already have one in mind, you can call on the way."

He phoned his mother first.

Escorting Indra into the police station, I felt like some '50s television dad bringing him downtown to apologize for a misguided prank. I was getting old enough that the clients, the suspects, the victims, they could all be my kids.

Indra was crying in the interview room when I left.

I dialed the new number my client had given me, explained the whole story, said I'd enclose a final report with my bill.

Tim rattled off a bunch of curses. "I feel like it's all my fault. If only I'd caught him red-handed, he'd still be alive. I'm the team leader. Why didn't Frank come to me?"

"The weight of love, family, and religion is not so easily calculated. There's no point blaming yourself for human excess."

"What a waste." From a clatter in the background I assumed the police had allowed the staff back into Berkshire Steakhouse. "What's going to happen to the kid who shot Frank?"

"That's for the courts to decide."

"I can't believe how this mushroomed."

"Something my father used to say when he pried me and my brother apart: 'Where's the beef?'"

"I don't get his point." Tim's voice sounded distracted.

"Our father was saying we were fighting over air. Words. "

"Yeah, well, I gotta go." There was a click, and Tim was gone.

Meet Author Stephen D. Rogers

Over five hundred of Stephen's stories and poems have appeared in more than two hundred publications, earning among other honors a Derringer (and five additional nominations), two "Notable Online Stories" from storySouth's Million Writers Award, honorable mention in "The Year's Best Fantasy and Horror," mention in "The Best American Mystery Stories," and numerous Readers' Choice awards.

Stephen is the Vice President of the New England Chapter, Mystery Writers of America, and the head writer at Crime Scene (online interactive mysteries). His website, www.stephendrogers.com, includes a list of new and upcoming titles as well as other timely information.

Use this form to order other chillingly good mysteries from Mainly Murder Press.

Title	Qty	Cover Price	Subtotal
Waiting for Armando-Ivie		$14.95	
Murder on Old Main St.-Ivie		$14.95	
A Skeleton in the Closet-Ivie		$14.95	
Moonlighting in Vermont-George		$14.95	
Maracaibo – Ciullo		$15.95	
25 Years Ago Today – Juba		$14.95	
Murder by Yew-- Young		$14.95	
		Subtotal:	
		CT residents add 6% tax	
		S&H $2.99 first book, $1.00 each additional	
		Total enclosed:	

Mail with your check and shipping instructions to:
Mainly Murder Press
PO Box 290586 • Wethersfield, CT 06109-0586

or use PayPal to order online at
www.MainlyMurderPress.com

LaVergne, TN USA
07 June 2010
185198LV00001B/14/P